DON'T!! STOP!!
THAT TICKLES!!

A Boner Book

DON'T!! STOP!!
THAT TICKLES!!

A Collection of Stories

FIRST EDITION

A Boner Book by
The Nazca Plains Corporation
Las Vegas, Nevada
2006

ISBN:1-887895-31-0

Published by:

The Nazca Plains Corporation ®
4640 Paradise Rd, Suite 141
Las Vegas NV 89109-8000

PUBLISHER'S NOTE
This is a work of fiction. Names, characters, places, and inci-dents either are the products of the writer's imagination or are used fictitiously, and any resemblance to actual persons, living or dead, business establishments, events or locales is entirely coincidental.

Cover Model, Travis Jay
Cover Photography by Corwin
Author Photograph by Don Ventura
Editor, Blake Stephens
Art Direction, Robert Steele

Introduction

It's funny, (no pun intended) but when I started writing foot fetish stories it was evident very quickly that most of the questions I was asked was about tickling a guy's feet. I came to realize that male foot fetish and tickling seemed to go hand in hand, or foot in hand, or however one prefers to see it. I was told by many of my foot fetish buddies and by people who had read my first two books, how "Nothing is better than tickling a studly guy's feet. Nothing is better than making a poor tied up guy laugh his head off." When I heard those things I of course had questions, obviously, I mean, I am a very inquisitive guy when it comes to men's feet. Okay, when you tickle a guy is it mandatory that he be tied up? If so, how do you go about convincing him to let you tie him up? Can I tickle his feet while he's wearing his socks? And so many other questions, like, what if his feet aren't ticklish? If his feet aren't ticklish can I tickle other parts of him instead that might be ticklish? Can I explore him until I find specific tickle points? Instead of definite answers all I got was more questions. As I thought about it I decided to try my hand (hands?) (No pun intended, ha, ha.) at writing some tickle tales. Thinking about it some more I decided to combine a few other fetishes into the stories that I would write in the tickle genre. I love playing on a guy's machismo when it comes to a gambling sort of challenge (as was done in one of my favorite books "That Day at The Quarry" by Tom Shaw) and I also love how ordinary household items can be turned into instruments of torture, items like a feather-duster or a toothbrush. With those things in mind I created "Tickled Yuppie." Other things I love where a guy's feet are concerned include one of the latest fashion statements in the world of baseball. What I am referring to here are those long dark colored socks, aptly called "High Socks" that tuck into a baseball player's uniform pants. A lot of baseball players nowadays seem to favor that style. That fetish combined with tickling caused my story "The Pitcher" to be born. Lastly, I love devices, or to be more precise, sinister devices, even fictional science fiction sort of devices. My story "Mr. Kujman's Device" incorporated that fetish and I came up with the idea for a tickle device…a tickle device that a handsome lawyer with an over-sized ego and big feet would unwittingly become the test subject for…

Happy Reading and I hope you get a laugh or two (or three or four) from my first book of tickle tales…

For Timmy and Vince...
(Two of the best tickle buddies a guy can know...)

Contents

1   TICKLED YUPPIE

17   THE PITCHER

45   MR. KUJMAN'S DEVICE

143   ABOUT THE AUTHOR

Tickled Yuppie

My name is Peter, Peter Berg to be exact. Christopher is one of my closest friends. He's also one of my kinkiest friends in the world. We've known each other for a lot of years but recently we got to know each other a little better. We're both twenty-six years old. I have light brown hair, brown eyes, and a pretty muscular body from working out regularly at the gym. I'm five feet ten inches tall. Christopher is slightly shorter than me. He has dark brown hair and brown sad looking eyes. His body is pretty lean from all the hours he spends on the exercise bike he owns. When Christopher called me at my office during the day and invited me over (after work) for some T.T. I had no idea what he was talking about; he would not even tell me what T.T. stood for. But because I was extremely curious I decided to accept the invitation. I arrived at Christopher's apartment wearing a Burberry navy blue business suit, a white shirt, a yellow silk paisley tie, and black wingtip shoes. Christopher greeted me at the door. He was wearing a pair of black shorts, a white tee shirt, and sneakers with no socks. He ushered me into the apartment and we sat down on the living room couch. Christopher handed me a cold beer and popped one open for himself also. We both took a long swallow of our beers and then I placed my beer can on the coffee table, removed my suit jacket, loosened my tie, and leaned back on the couch. I crossed one leg on my knee and looked at Christopher.

"Okay Friend," I began with a grin on my face. "You

invited me over here for some T.T. and wouldn't tell me on the phone what T.T. is. Now, tell me, what is T.T.?"

Christopher smiled and put his beer can on the coffee table next to mine. He placed a hand on my ankle and moved his hand under my pants leg, toying with my sock. He looked into my eyes and said "tickle torture."

My eyes lit up and I laughed.
"Tickle torture?" I asked him. "You're going to tickle torture me?"

"Or maybe you'll tickle torture me," Christopher replied.

My curiosity was more than piqued.
"Okay, I'm game, but how do we decide who gets tickle tortured?" I asked Christopher anxiously.

Christopher moved his hand over my wingtip and toyed with the laces, tugging on them. He thought for a moment and then said, "We'll make it a game. The loser of the game gets tied up and tickled." Now it was my turn to think it over. Tied up??? I had never been tied up in my whole life and didn't plan to start now. I mean, even when I was a kid and my friends and I played cops and robbers I was always the cop. I never got tied up. But still, there was the possibility that I would win the game and get to tie up Christopher. Now that sounded like fun. I finally agreed and asked what kind of a game we would play to decide who would get tied up and tickle tortured. At that, Christopher took his hand off my wingtip (reluctantly it seemed), reached under the couch, and produced a deck of playing cards. He shuffled them a few times and placed them on the coffee table facedown.

"Okay," Christopher said as he was about to explain. "We each take one card out of the deck. The guy with the lower value card gets tickle tortured."

"That's the game?" I asked in shock.

"Yup Yuppie, nice and easy, and quick huh?"

Christopher teased, tugging on my tie. "I can't wait to get started tickle torturing you Friend."

I put my foot down on the floor, and feeling pretty confident reached into the deck of cards and pulled out a card. Christopher did the same thing. We looked at our cards and then looked at each other expectantly.

"Let's do it together," Christopher instructed.

I nodded in agreement and we placed our cards on the coffee table face up. Christopher's card was an ace of hearts. My card was a king of diamonds.

"Wow," I said dejectedly. "For a whole second there I thought I would have won with that king."

"Nope, looks to me like you lose," Christopher said and grabbed my necktie and pulled me close to him. "Let's get started. I have everything ready in the bedroom."

I gulped as Christopher lifted my feet into his lap, untied my wingtips, and I didn't do anything as he yanked them off my feet. My heart pounded as Christopher squeezed my socked feet a few times. At that moment I sadly realized what I had gotten myself into, I also thought about how very ticklish I really was, but shit, there was no turning back now. I had agreed to the rules of the game after all. Christopher and I stood up, facing each other. Christopher undid my necktie and unbuttoned my shirt. I stood there totally docile. In what seemed like seconds I was bare chested. I breathed heavily as Christopher squeezed one of my nipples.

"Been spending a lot of time at the gym eh?"

Christopher asked me, my nipple pinched between his thumb and first two fingers as he looked at my big muscular chest.

"Yeah, I guess," I replied breathlessly as Christopher twisted my nipple a bit.

"Looks good," my buddy said and took his fingers off my nipple and proceeded to squeeze one of my bowling ball-sized biceps. "Now for your pants…"

I watched as Christopher undid my belt and unlatched my suit pants. They fell down around my ankles. As I grudgingly stepped out of my pants Christopher picked up my necktie.

"You have to be blindfolded," Christopher told me. "I didn't mention it earlier but it is part of the rules."

"I'll bet that if I had won you wouldn't have told me that," I said with a grin.

I stood still as Christopher stepped behind me and tied my tie over my eyes. That done, he held me by one arm and guided me slowly to the bedroom, noticing that my manhood was hard as a rock in my Botany 500 white briefs.

"Looks to me like you're enjoying this," Christopher said.

We got to the bedroom and Christopher stretched me out on the bed on my back in a spread eagle position. I felt the first rope being wound around my wrist and then tied to the "headboard. My heart pounded like crazy in my chest.

"I want a chance to get even later on," I said.

As Christopher tied my other wrist he laughed at me and said, "With your luck you'll probably lose the game again and wind up getting doubly tickle tortured tonight."

"Maybe not..." I replied as I felt a rope being wound tightly around one of my socked feet.

"Do you really want to take the chance?" Christopher asked me as he ran a finger over the bottom of my now bound foot.

My leg jerked a bit and I chuckled.

"I'll decide for sure after you've had your fun," I replied.

Christopher grabbed my other socked foot and tied it to the bedpost on that side of the bed. I was now trapped, wearing only my white briefs and black socks. Christopher began running a finger over my nipples, my hips, and stomach areas. I chuckled softly at first and laughed harder as Christopher increased the tempo and the speed of his finger as it trailed over my nakedness.

"Having fun?" Christopher asked me. "It sure sounds like you are..."

"Go ahead," I laughed. "Ha, ha, ha, ha, my turn comes later..."

"Maybe," Christopher said as he began running his fingers over my crotch and thighs.

I whooped out my laughter and struggled furiously against the ropes as I laughed harder and harder.

"Glad you accepted my invitation Peter?" Christopher asked me mockingly.

I was unable to reply because by now I was laughing hysterically as Christopher tickled the bottom of one of my feet.

"This is nothing yet Friend," Christopher laughed. "Wait till I get the feather duster."

"Y-you wouldn't, ha, ha, ha, ha, ha, ha, ha, y-you wouldn't..." I said hysterically.

"Oh yes I would," Christopher answered. "Then I'm going to take your socks off your feet and run a dry toothbrush over them..."

I sputtered and saliva dripped from my lips as Christopher went to work tickling my other foot.
"We've only begun Peter," Christopher said. "Wait'll I flip you over onto your stomach. We're going to find out just how ticklish your ass cheeks are."

I could only laugh and listen as Christopher told me his fiendish plans for me.

Fifteen minutes later Christopher stopped tickling me. He told me that I could have a five minute break to catch my breath. He took the blindfold off me and sat down on the bed next to me. I was already drenched in sweat as I smiled up at my friend.

"I hope you're enjoying torturing me, because pretty soon you'll be the one tied to this damned bed," I said and tugged on the ropes.

"You keep saying that, but remember the rules my friend…" Christopher replied and squeezed one of my nipples hard, getting a good loud gasp out of me. "If you draw a losing card you'll wind up back where you started."

I licked my lips and asked for a drink. Christopher went to the living room an came back with one of the beers. He put it to my mouth and I drank.

"Thank you," I said.

I watched as Christopher put the beer down on a night table and then he reached under the bed and produced a large feather duster.

"Oh shit," I murmured.

Christopher checked his watch and told me that my five minutes were up. He blindfolded me again and began by tickling my chest with the feather duster. I let out a few sneezes in between hysterical bouts of laugher. A few minutes later my so called buddy ripped my briefs off me. My hard-on pointed at the ceiling.

"What a boner!" Christopher said jovially.

Before I could reply or even object to the fact that he had ripped my briefs off me Christopher was running the feather duster over my cock and balls and I was laughing and sweating profusely.

"Pl-please stop," I begged, laughing at the same time.

"No way," Christopher said. "The game must continue."

Christopher grew bored of the feather duster and tossed it on the floor. He then sat down on my huge muscular chest, straddling me.

"What now?" I asked him.

"Armpits," Christopher replied with a grin.

"OH NO!!" I yelled.

Without the slightest hesitation Christopher placed each of his hands under one of my hairy armpits and with his finger-tips tickled them furiously. I squealed with sudden uncontrollable laughter.

"I-I can't take it!!" I screamed. "PLEASE STOP, ha, ha, ha, ha, ha, ha, ha, ha, ha, ha!!!"

But Christopher ignored me and kept on tickling and tickling me. I felt Christopher's hard-on against my chest. I knew then just where this was going to lead and why Christopher had really wanted me there that night. My thoughts were cut off however as another burst of hysterical laughter escaped me.

"Please stop tickling my pits!!" I begged.

"You should try to enjoy this Peter, because the time is coming close when I'm going to take your socks off you and tickle your bare feet with a toothbrush," Christopher said. "It's going to be much worse than having your armpits tickled."

Finally, Christopher did stop tickling my armpits. He climbed off the bed and picked up the feather duster again. He ran the duster over my thighs. I squirmed on the bed and laughed hard and loud.

"What'll you do to make me stop Peter?" Christopher inquired.

So that was it. I had known it as soon as I felt Christopher's hard-on. I answered Christopher's question with another question... "What would you want me to do?" Suddenly, Christopher stopped tickling my thighs and leaned over my face. He lowered my blindfold.

"Let's start with a kiss," Christopher demanded, making suggestive movements with his lips and tongue.

I pulled my face away.

"Are you nuts?" I yelled. "I'm not queer!"

"Who said anything about being queer?" Christopher asked.

"I won't kiss you!" I shouted.

Christopher shrugged and picked up the feather duster. "Oh well, looks like I'll just have to tickle you some more," he said as he blindfolded me again.

"Alright, alright!!" I said, not believing what I said next. "I'll fucking kiss you."

I could actually feel Christopher smiling. He leaned down and pressed his mouth against mine. To his surprise I responded by shoving my tongue forcefully and deep into Christopher's mouth. He put one hand behind my neck and squeezed gently as we kissed. Pre cum was oozing from my piss hole. When the kiss was done Christopher stood up and resumed tickling my thighs with the feather duster.

"HEY!!!" I yelped. "You promised you would stop tickling me if I kissed you!!"

"I never promised anything Peter," Christopher responded. "Besides, it'll take more than a kiss to make me stop tickling you."

Once again I was trapped in a hysterical bout of laughter.

Christopher finally stopped tickling my thighs about fifteen minutes later. By now I was breathless, sweaty, and thirsty.

"Let's take another break," Christopher said.

Once again he lowered my blindfold and gave me a few sips of beer.

"Having fun?" Christopher asked me.

"Tons of it," I responded sarcastically. "How much longer are you going to tickle me for?"

Christopher told me that we had a way to go yet. Then he smiled down at me and told me that another kiss might, just might, take ten minutes off my tickle torture time. Without any hesitation, I said, "Okay, kiss me," and opened my mouth. Christopher leaned down and we kissed long and hard again, our tongues exploring and probing in each other's mouth. When the kiss ended we looked at each other passionately and Christopher gently squeezed one of my nipples.

"What happens next?" I asked him.

Christopher regained his composure and walked to the foot of the bed. I watched as he untied my feet and slowly peeled my black dress socks off me, tossing them on the floor.

"Oh no," I whispered.

"Oh yes," Christopher said as he retied my feet to the posts of the bed.

I saw Christopher take a toothbrush out from under the bed and then he blindfolded me again. Christopher knelt at the foot of the bed and began running the toothbrush bristles over the bottom of my right foot.

"OH GOD, ha, ha, ha, ha, ha, ha, ha, please stop!!" I shrieked.

Christopher alternated from one of my feet to the other with the toothbrush. I jerked spasmodically on the bed, howling with laughter.

"What will you do to make me stop this time?" Christopher asked.

"Wh-what do you want me to do, kiss you again?" I asked in return.

The tickling intensified and so did my laughter.

"It's going to take more than a kiss to stop me this time Peter," Christopher said and tickled me some more.

"HA HA HA HA HA HA HA HA OHHHH GOD, tell me what you fucking want!!" I begged.

I knew at that moment that Christopher felt triumphant. "Suck my cock," Christopher announced.

Christopher stopped tickling me, I stopped laughing, and the room was eerily silent all of a sudden.

Moments later, Christopher was sitting in a chair, naked. I was kneeling before him, sucking and slurping on his huge cock. I was untied and my blindfold was hanging loosely around my neck.

"Oh yeah, that feels so fucking good," Christopher panted as he caressed the back of my neck.

I sucked, kissed, and licked Christopher's cock and balls.

"Looks to me like you're enjoying all of this Peter," Christopher teased me.

I stopped and looked up at my friend.

"It's better than being tickle tortured," I said.

Christopher grabbed his cock and pushed it back into my mouth. I quickly resumed sucking him.

"You still have some tickling to endure my friend," he said. "Remember, I still haven't worked on your ass yet. The game isn't over yet."

Then, Christopher pulled his cock out of my mouth and shot his load, squirting his juices all over my chest. The cum was hot and it dripped slowly toward my stomach area and my pubic bush.

"What a hefty load!!" I remarked.

"Yeah," Christopher agreed, panting as he spoke. "Later on we'll see how much you shoot. Now, back to the game!" In moments I was tied to the bed again, on my stomach this time, and blindfolded.

"Welcome to the end of the game Friend," Christopher said. "The tickling of your ass!"

"Please take it easy," I said.

Using the feather duster Christopher began tickling my ass cheeks. Once again I began howling and squealing with laughter. Christopher laughed as my sexy ass bounced up and down on the bed. He laughed even harder when I farted.

"Please stop!" I yelled. "Let's end the game now!!"

"Only when you tell me what you'll do to make me stop," Christopher replied.

I now knew what Christopher wanted. I told him to stop tickling me and to go ahead and make me cum.

"I thought you'd never ask," Christopher said.

He tickled my ass cheeks a little more and then it happened. He tossed the feather duster aside and reached under my crotch, pulling my cock and balls out from under me.

"AAARRR!!!" I yelled as Christopher lay down between my legs and took my hardness in his mouth.

He sucked my cock furiously and then I shot my load, squirting it all over the bed sheets.

"Congratulations Peter, you've survived the T.T. game," Christopher announced.

Sure, but I still wanted my chance to get even. After all, it wasn't everyday that I allowed someone to do this to me. Christopher untied me and took the blindfold off me. Later, we were both dressed and sitting in the living room drinking another beer each.

"That was some game," I said. "But how about my chance to get even?"

"Are you sure you want to take that chance Friend?" Christopher asked me warningly. "After all, you do know the rules."

A look of smug confidence came over my face.

"Shuffle the cards…Friend," I said.

Christopher did. We each drew a card. Christopher drew a three of hearts and I drew a two of clubs.

"Shit, shit, shit…" I whimpered as Christopher jumped to his feet and danced around the room, laughing mockingly.

"I cannot believe it!!" Christopher taunted me. "I cannot fucking believe your bad luck!!"

"Neither can I…" I muttered woefully.

"C'mon Peter, strip for me again, strip down to your socks and lets get started tickling you again," Christopher spouted joyfully.

Moments later I was stripped and blindfolded as Christopher led me back to the bedroom.

"Looks like it's going to be a long night…" Christopher said as he held my arm tight.

Tickling The Pitcher

Authors Note and Dedication:

This story has been revised from a previous tickle torture story I wrote starring a celebrity baseball player. In this rewrite the name of the baseball player has been changed and modified, but readers should still be able to pick up on who is being referred to herein…

I don't know all the rules of baseball so I don't know if a team can win a game based on a pitcher's throw. But I needed that in this story as an excuse for the star baseball player (the pitcher) to be carried off the field by his teammates. Also, I have been told that when a baseball player causes the win of a game it is a tradition to hoist him on his teammates shoulders and carry him off the field in celebration. Numerous guys that play baseball on neighborhood or college teams that I have chatted with have told me what an awesome feeling it is to cause the win of a game, and then to be carried off the field. Seeing your teammates coming toward you, embracing you, and then the lucky ones who squat down to get their hands around your legs and calves, unbelievable feeling as your feet leave the ground. More than a few guys have also told me how they found that they were hard and very aroused as they were carried off the field. One guy said that as just one of his team-mates had him up on his shoulders he felt his hardness pressing against his buddies' neck as he lugged him across the field, amid the cheers and applause of the crowd that had gathered to see the game. If his buddy carrying him noticed it or felt it against the back of his neck he didn't make mention of it or elaborate on it. Guys have also told me how they felt very vulnerable and powerless being balanced up there so awkwardly on their buddy or buddies shoulders, and that was what I wanted for the purposes of this story, at the end when the pitcher is carried back into the locker room by his so-called adoring fans. He feels more than vulnerable, perilously balanced up there. The next time you see a baseball player being carried off the field note the expression of triumph mixed with slight nervousness etched on his face. Another buddy of mine once said that it is to spotlight the guy when his buddies carry him off the field, responding to a question I had asked on the subject matter. I also don't know if there really is a legend that decrees if you lick a great baseball player's feet you too will become a great baseball player. I'm sure more than a few of us foot fiends would love the opportunity to find out though, just to have an excuse to lick some handsome baseball guy's stinking feet...

This story is dedicated with love and appreciation to my good buddy Jim in Florida... Happy Reading Jim!!!

"Ha, ha, ha, ha, ha, ha, ha, ha, ha, ha, ha, ha!!!!!!!" laughed the great baseball player "Cooba", as his teammates had nicknamed him, as my four buddies and I took turns tickling his navy blue socked feet. "Th-this is terrible, ohhhrrrr g-gads, ha, ha, ha, ha, ha, th-this is no way to be treating a world famous baseball player! I swear, when I get myself untied you guys are going to be more than sorry! Ha, ha, ha, ha, ha, ha, ha, ha, ha, ha, ha, ha!!!! Ohhhhhrrrrrr , my god!!!"

"The way we got you tied good and tight I don't see that happening any time soon oh great one," Rodd chuckled and quickly slurped "Cooba's" smelly socked toes back into his mouth.

"Gawd, ohhhhhhhhrrrr gads, f-fucking guys are t-tickling me and, and, ha, ha, ha, ha, ha, ha, ha, ha, s-sucking my stinking toes too!!! Ha, ha, ha, ha, ha, ha, ha!!!!"

As Rodd sucked the baseball player's toes Angel tickle tortured the bottom of the guy's foot. The sounds of "Cooba's" laughter echoed loudly in the deserted locker room. Luck had been on our side when it turned out that our favorite player on our hometown team was the last one in the locker room that day. My four buddies and I had always admired the great pitcher "Cooba", as I said, nicknamed by his teammates. Not just the great way he pitched in the game, but also that tight fitting baseball uniform he wore, all the way down to those long navy blue socks that he wore, with his uniform pants tucked tightly over them. My buddies and I always said that "Cooba" shows a lot of sock! Oh yeah, my buddies and I really wanted to get our mouths and hands on those feet of "Cooba's." (Not to mention other parts of his muscular mocha colored body as well.) So many times we had talked about it and fantasized and came up with fiendish ideas on how to land the great baseball player. We even made jokes about licking the top of his sweaty baldhead after a good hard game out in the sun. No doubt the pitcher's dome would be more than sweaty and smelly, having worn his cap throughout most of the game. It would be Rodd who achieved that honor on the day we landed the great baseball player. Rodd always said that there was something real kinky and hot about licking a handsome guy's baldhead. Yeah, fucking "Cooba" drove us wild that were for sure! When Dennis got us all tickets to the game for that Saturday night it was decided. Somehow or other we would get into the player's locker room after the game. If we couldn't land "Cooba" and if we were caught in the locker room we would simply say that we wanted an autograph from some of our favorite baseball players on our favorite baseball team.

"Damn, his feet really do stink," Dennis quipped, his mouth and nose pressed firmly against the bottom of one of "Cooba's" navy blue socked feet.

"He just went nine innings in the hot grueling sun," I said with a grin. "Fucking game lasted more than four hours into the early evening. You expect his socks to smell spring fresh or something?"

Holding his raised foot by the ankle we tickle tortured the bottom of his foot with our fingertips.

"Ha, ha, ha, ha, ha, ha, ha, ha, ha!!!!" the baseball player roared uncontrollably. "Damned trouble makers!! What the hell kind of fans are you anyway??? Trap a baseball player in the locker room after the game and tickle torture him??? Shit, shit!! Ha, ha, ha, ha, ha, ha, ha, ha, ha, ha, ha, ha, ha!!!!!"

The sounds of our slurping at the baseball player's socks and feet drove us wild. The scent of those raunchy socks and feet of his made us wild for more and more. We weren't planning on letting him loose any time soon.

"Ha, ha, ha, ha, ha, ha, ha, ha, ha, ha, ha!!!" "Cooba" chortled. "Th-that legend you told me about earlier is bullshit you guys. Ha, ha, ha, ha, ha, ha, ha, ha, ha, ha!!!! You guys were just looking for an excuse to get me into this damned position!!"

"And we got you oh great one," Dennis laughed.

So, armed with rope in our backpacks we sat through the long game in the hot sun until early evening. Our team won and we watched as "Cooba" was carried off the field by a few of his fellow players. It had been his pitch that had won the game for them. The team members carrying our favorite player off the field had their hands wrapped tightly around his navy blue socked ankles as he sat aloft on their shoulders. Needless to say our hearts pounded. Jealous? You bet your ass we were jealous. We would have given anything to be the guys carrying that fucking stud on our shoulders and have our hands wrapped around those long socks of his. (The five of us, as we had all been buddies for some time had all discovered that we had a kinky foot fetish.) At that moment we could only imagine how great those socks of "Cooba's" stunk. We figured that being that "Cooba" was the hero of this particular game he would be the last guy out of the locker room. He would have to stay around for the champagne baths and the claps on the back and the slaps on the ass he was in for. No doubt his fellow players would take turns riding the guy around the locker room on their shoulders. We were sure that none of them would celebrate his great game the way we wanted to celebrate it, to tie the handsome fuck up real tight and tickle torture the very bejesus out of him. Later, outside the locker room we saw a few players at a time emerging, dressed in street clothes. Some fans waited outside for autographs and the players happily obliged them. When we didn't see the great "Cooba" emerge from the locker room we knew we were in luck. We waited till we had counted off just about all the team members, silently hoping and praying that "Cooba" would remain last and alone in the locker room. When the last of the team members came out of the locker room we dashed to the door before it could close and lock. With our hearts thundering in our chest we entered the locker room of our hometown baseball team. Like any other locker room it reeked of sweat, man sweat, baseball player sweat to be exact. The scent of champagne also wafted in the air. We walked past the bathroom and the scent of baseball player piss assaulted our nostrils and made our nuts churn. In the shower area we saw discarded towels and jock straps. The scent from in there was just as hot as the pissy scented bathroom. As we walked slowly through the rows of lockers we saw him. He was sitting on a long bench in front of his locker with his muscular back to us. Oh man, of fuck, the great "Cooba" I thought wildly and breathed hard the musty scent of the locker room of the world famous baseball team. He was wearing just the lower portion of his baseball uniform complete with his cleats and those long navy blue socks of his. We all looked at each other and gave a unanimous thumbs-up. We approached him silently. He was sitting in front of his locker, still all sweaty from the game, sipping a bottle of cold mineral water, a bottle of champagne on the floor at his feet. He hadn't showered yet. Great! He looked beat and the sound of his breathing was labored. Even greater! It would be easy to land him and get him roped up for our fun. He put the bottle of mineral water down on the floor and picked up the champagne. He chugged it heartily. He reeked of the stuff too. No doubt his fellow players had liberally showered him with the stuff after and probably during carrying him into the locker room. I hoped that he had drunk enough of the stuff to dull his wits just a little (a lot?) for us. We saw that his back was very muscular, well chiseled and glistening with sweat as he leaned back on the bench and chugged the champagne.

"Cooba," my buddy Dennis, the ringleader and whose idea this had been said.

The baseball player turned around and saw us, five guys in their early twenties standing there, all of us holding autograph books in our hands. That was our excuse for being in the locker room.

"Hey there," he said with that great grin of his and got to his feet and faced us, balancing himself on his cleats. "How did you guys get in here? This locker room is supposed to be off limits to the fans."

He put the bottle of champagne down on the floor next to his bottle of mineral water.

"I mean, you are fans, right?" the baseball player asked us. "You're not fans of that opposing team we just bested are you?"

"No Sir Cooba, you see, the door was open and when we asked where you were the guy outside told us you were still in here," Dennis explained quickly, the blond guy being a mischief-maker for as long as I could recall. "We were hoping we could all get your autograph "Cooba.""

"And which guy would that be?" "Cooba" asked us, knowing that Dennis was lying through his teeth.

"Uh, I, uh, forgot his name," Dennis replied as the great baseball player stared him down.

He was standing there sopped in sweat, fucking tall guy that he is, grinning from ear to ear, his pride elevated that some fans actually snuck into the locker room just to get his autograph.

He was beautifully muscled and more than well chiseled. His skin was the color of mocha, smooth, and his chest big and jutting out with two big brown fleshy nipples adorning it. "Cooba's" belly button was deep and wide, made for tickling. His head was bald, not a hair on it. I guessed that he had it shaved and shined every other day or so. Man, I knew that Rodd would have loved to have the pleasure of being "Cooba's" barber. No doubt my good buddy would spend an inordinate amount of time rubbing the lotion on the baseball player's dome. Fuck, the great pitcher was good looking in a way that drove us all wild with kinky lust. His smooth skin was bathed and glistening in smelly man sweat. Fuck it all man, he smelled awesome.

"Well then, I suppose there's nothing wrong with that," the baseball player said and reached for Dennis' book that he was holding.

As soon as the baseball player's arm was outstretched and his armpit visible Alex and Ross made their move. They grabbed "Cooba's" arm, pushed it up and pressed their finger-tips deep into his sweaty mangy pit, swirling them around in there.

"H-hey, ha, ha, ha, ha, ha, ha, ha, ha, ha, ha, ha, ha, ha, ha!!!!!" Wh-what do you fellas th-think you're doing?" the great baseball player gasped and chortled in surprise. "Ha, ha, ha, ha, ha, ha, ha, ha, ha, ha, ha!!!!"

As he moved his other arm to try and ward them off Angel and Dennis quickly grabbed his other arm, pushed it up and set to work tickling the guy's other sweaty stinky pit. "Ha, ha, ha, ha, ha, ha, ha, ha, ha, ha, ha, ha, ha!!!! Oh shit, wh-what is this, some kind of prank?" "Cooba" rasped, his muscular arms flailing uselessly out at his sides over my four buddies heads.

He stood there laughing and all befuddled with sweat fly-ing off his exquisite body as all four of my buddies really dug deep into his pits.

"Har, har, har, har, har, ha, ha, ha, ha, ha, ha, ha, ha!!!!" "Cooba's" voice boomed loudly through the locker room as he backed up against his locker.

He tried grabbing at the guys to pry them off him, but it was no use. Every time he moved a hand toward one of them another of them simply pushed it away. "Cooba" was going to be tickle tortured, whether he submitted to it or not bud. He must have felt like a guy trapped by a pack of octopi the way my buddies kept grappling with him, tickling him more and more and more. The baseball player had obviously consumed lots of champagne. I stepped forward and trailed my fingertips over his sides, stomach area and deep into his belly button. "Ohhhhhhhrrrrr, ha, ha, ha, ha, ha, ha, ha, ha, ha, ha, ha, ha, ha, ha oh please you guys!!" the baseball player gasped, sweating more and more now. "Fun's fun but this is too much!! Ha, ha, ha, ha, ha, ha, ha, ha, ha, ha!!!!!"

His face was lit up in a forced smile and grimace as we tickled and tickled the fuck out of him. Every time he tried to get at us with one of his arms we quickly pushed the arm away again and tickled him harder and harder. He did an uncontrolled and stupid looking dance in front of his locker as we tickled him still harder and harder, trying his damnedest to stay balanced on his cleats. Within moments the great baseball player had been reduced to a laughing mess of quivering Jell-O. Then, Dennis and Alex's backpacks slid from their backs and they looked at me intently. I nodded knowingly. As I opened Alex's backpack he and Dennis yanked the baseball player's muscular arms up behind him and held them together tightly at the wrists.

"Wh-what are you guys up to?" "Cooba" asked, now able to speak coherently as we (temporarily) stopped tickling him.

He was helpless and winded as Alex and Dennis forcefully turned him around so that I could get at his wrists. "Shit, what are you guys tying me up for?" the baseball player asked in a panic as I expertly roped his wrists tightly behind him. "All this for a damned autograph???"

"We want a lot more than your autograph "Cooba",
Dennis quipped, looking hungrily at the baseball player's sweat
soaked chest. "We want to have some mean fun with you."

"M-mean fun?" the great pitcher croaked. "Just what the
hell do you mugs have in mind for me here?"

Daring as ever Dennis took a quick slurp at one of
"Cooba's" big fleshy nipples. The guy shivered, as chills no
doubt coursed through his magnificent body. He looked quizzi-
cally at Dennis for all of a split second, no doubt wondering
why some guy fan would want to steal a slurp at one of his
nips. When his hands were tied well and tight we all hoisted
him and got him down on his stomach on the long bench he
had been sitting on when we found him. Dennis and Alex held
the guy's big feet up off the bench by his ankles, as the other
three of us got busy roping him quickly to the bench.

"Wh-what is going on here?" the great "Cooba" seethed
as we roped him to the bench.

"There's an old legend," Dennis said, holding one of
"Cooba's" ankles tight and unlacing his cleat.

"And what the fuck is that?" "Cooba" asked as his cleat
was taken off his foot.

"The legend is that if a person gets the chance to lick a
great baseball player's stinking feet then they too will become a
great baseball player," Dennis said, pressing his nose and
mouth against the bottom of "Cooba's" navy blue socked foot.
"And may I say for the record Sir that your feet sure do stink."
We all laughed merrily as we finished getting the great baseball
player's upper torso roped tight to the bench. He grimaced mis-

erably as his other cleat slid off his foot courtesy of Dennis. "Cooba's" feet scent wafted up at us as and filled the air we were breathing. Good God, his feet really did fucking stink, even worse than we ever imagined. All those times watching him on television and thinking and talking about licking his smelly feet, wondering just how bad his feet ranked, now my buddies and I had our chance. Fuck, we had the great "Cooba's" big feet right in our faces for Christ's sake. The guy was perilously balanced on and tied tight on the bench, stretched out nice and long on his stomach, his legs held in the air by his ankles by Dennis. Dennis stole sniffs and licks at "Cooba's" raised feet. "Cooba" watched as we passed his stinking cleats around, sniffing heartily at the moist insides of them. They smelled all hot and musty. Just the way a great baseball player's cleats should stink at the end of a long game in the hot sun.

"Damned practical jokers," he seethed through clenched teeth. "Used autographs as an excuse to get in here, tickled me to get the drop on me and now you five got me roped up good and fucking tight. And look at you perverts, sniffing the inside of my smelly shoes. That guy up there licking and kissing my rank toes, fuck, horrible way to treat a baseball player of my stature. Legend my foot."

"But "Cooba", we really do want to lick your stinking feet," Dennis said and slid the tip of his tongue over the bottom of "Cooba's" raised feet. "And who knows, maybe licking your feet we will become great baseball players."

"Oh God," "Cooba" said in total disbelief.

At that Dennis trailed his fingertips over the bottom of the trapped baseball player's socked feet.

"Ha, ha, ha, ha, ha, ha, ha, ha, ha, ha, ha, ha, ha, ha!!!"

the great baseball player guffawed wildly. "Fuck man, don't be tickling my stinking feet you guys!!"

That said we all laughed loudly. I quickly roped "Cooba's" legs together just above his long socks and then we all went to work tickling his raised feet and licking his socks all over. We drooled over his socks and quickly lapped up our saliva. We sucked his moist and stinking socked toes, kissed his ankles and tickled him more and more.

"Ha, ha, ha, ha, ha, ha, ha, ha, ha, ha, ha, ha, ha, ha, ha!!!!!!" "Cooba" cackled, his deep voice bouncing off the walls of the locker room as we did our dirty work. "L-lousy trick to have played on me you guys!! Ha, ha, ha, ha, ha, ha, ha, ha, ha, ha, ha, ha, ha, ha, ha, ha, ha, ha, ha!!!!!"

Louder and louder he laughed…

Dennis picked up the bottle of champagne that "Cooba" had been chugging when we found him. He poured some of it over the baseball player's feet as Alex and I held his feet up by his ankles.

"A little celebration for us too guys," Dennis said and Alex and I quickly went to work sucking at the baseball player's champagne socked toes.

"G-gads, crazy guys are sucking my damned stinking toes, and through my rancid socks of all things," "Cooba" seethed in disbelief.

He didn't seethe all that long because as Alex and I sucked his toes the other guys resumed tickling his feet, all of them running their fingertips over the meaty bottoms of them. "Ha, ha, ha, ha, ha, ha, ha, ha, ha, ha, ha, ha, ha, ha, ha, ha!!!!" "Cooba" chortled anew.

"When we're done here I'm keeping these smelly socks of his as a souvenir of this," Dennis quipped and snapped one of "Cooba's" socks against his leg.

"F-fuck man, you can have my damned socks!" the great baseball player chortled angrily. "J-just let me out of this, ha, ha, ha, ha, ha, ha, ha, ha, ha, ha!!!!! Ohhhrrrrr Gods!!!"

As "Cooba" laughed uncontrollably Rodd poured the contents of a champagne bottle he had found in "Cooba's" locker over the trapped baseball player's baldhead.

"Ohhhhhhrrrr shit," the guy grumbled angrily as he was showered with champagne and tickled at the same time.

"Man oh man, when they carried him off the field I just knew we would have our favorite baseball player in this position!" Dennis said and kissed the bottom of "Cooba's" stinking feet over and over. "Damn, I love this guy's big feet!"

"F-favorite player?" the baseball player grumbled more than angrily. "Th-this is some fucking way to be treating your favorite player!!"

Rodd leaned down over "Cooba's" champagne sopped baldhead and slathered his big tongue over the top of it as the rest of us went to town tickling the baseball player's socked feet.

"Ha, ha, ha, ha, ha, ha, ha, ha, ha, ha, ha, ha, ha, ha, ha!!!" the great baseball player chortled loudly. "F-fucking guys are dr-driving me crazy!!! Ha, ha, ha, ha, ha, ha, ha, ha, ha, ha, ha, ha, ha, ha, ha!!!!!!"

Rodd poured more champagne over "Cooba's" head and

licked that off as well as we went on and on tickling his feet and licking them in between tickling and tickling them.

"Ohhhhhrrrrrr Gods, ha, ha, ha, ha, ha, ha, ha, ha, ha, ha, ha!!!!" the guy ranted. "H-how long do you g-guys plan on k-keeping this shit up???"

"Heh, if you only knew," Dennis laughed and stole a long wet slurp on the great "Cooba's" socked smelly toes. "Mmmmm, tastes nasty…"

About twenty minutes or so later we had "Cooba" sitting up on the long bench his hands still tied behind his back and his smelly navy blue socks off his feet now, courtesy of Dennis. Man, you never saw one guy take another guy's socks off his feet so slowly and so damned ceremoniously. Dennis slid those socks off "Cooba" like they were worth millions of dollars, actually to Dennis that was just what they worth. "Cooba's" long socks hung out of the back pocket of Dennis' jeans, a real raunchy souvenir of the whole experience. Rodd was sitting behind the great baseball player, holding the guy pressed up against himself as he went on and on slathering his tongue over his baldhead. He forced the baseball player to guzzle long gulps of champagne, keeping him slightly drunk at that point and very, very cooperative for us. Dennis and Alex were squatted down on the sides of the bench, holding one of "Cooba's" bare feet in each of their hands, tickle torturing the hell out of the meaty bottoms of them, driving the poor guy insane with laughter.

"Ha, ha, ha, ha, ha, ha, ha, ha, ha, ha, ha, ha!!!" the great baseball player laughed madly. "St-stop this already you guys!!!! Ha, ha, ha, ha, ha, ha, ha, ha, ha, ha, ha, ha!!!! Ohhhhrrrr gads, fucking guys are tickling me while this dude behind me is lick-licking my baldhead and feeding me cheap champagne!!! Ha, ha, ha, ha, ha, ha, ha, ha, ha, ha, ha, ha, ha!!!!!"

"Cooba" chortled and gasped in shock when Angel and I knelt down on the sides of his chest and slurped one of his big nipples each into our mouths.

"Ha, ha, ha, ha, ha, ha, ha, ha, ha, ha, ha, ha, ha, ha, ohhhhrrrrrrr!!!! Pl-please st-stop!!!" he pleaded desperately. None of us had mentioned the big tent that "Cooba's" cock (definitely of the jumbo size, judging from the bulge in his uniform pants) was making in his sweat and champagne soaked and stained uniform pants. Obviously though the guy was getting off on what we were doing to him. Either that or he had to piss like a racehorse. Probably both I guessed.

"Ha, ha, ha, ha, ha, ha, ha, ha, ha, ha, ha, ha, ha, ha, ha, oooooooooooooooooooooo ha, ha, ha, ha, ha, ha, ha, ha, ha!!!!!!" the great baseball player laughed uncontrollably as Dennis and Alex held his bare feet tight and meanly ran their fingertips against the moist bottoms of them.

So there was the great "Cooba", stretched out on a locker room bench, tied up, having his bare feet tickled, his nipples sucked, being forced fed champagne and having his baldhead licked, all courtesy of five of his die hard fans. Granted it was a shitty way for a group of fans to treat a baseball player they admired, but at the same time it was the only way for a group of fans to treat their baseball hero. His cock pounded long and hard in his baseball uniform pants and he laughed and laughed and laughed and laughed and laughed… When Dennis decided we were going to tie the guy down to a massage table in the locker room and tickle torture other parts of his body "Cooba" complained bitterly in the drunken stupor we had sent him into. We hoisted the guy up off the bench and he swore like a captured marine as we carried him across the locker room…

"Fucking scheming kids," the baseball guy seethed as we lugged him stretched out between the five of us. "Fuck, put me down and get out of here already!!!"

In what seemed like no time we had the guy stretched out on the padded massage table. He wasn't at all happy about the fact that we tied his arms in a stretched out position to the hasps on the nearby lockers, exposing his very bushy very ticklish armpits. Rodd did the honors of taking "Cooba's" uniform pants and jock strap off him as he and Alex stretched the baseball player's long legs out, binding them at the ankles to the locker hasps as well.

"N-no, oh Gods no, d-don't be stripping me now too you mugs!!" the great pitcher complained.

Alex and Rodd stole big sucks on the guy's big toes after tying him well and fucking tight. The baseball player's cock was of the jumbo size, pointing straight up at the ceiling of the locker room. It was long, thick and beefy, oozing more than a mess of pre cum and beads upon beads of baseball player piss. Fuck, it looked like it was hurting him the way he was so damned hard. I breathlessly wondered how many loads I could suck out of the great baseball player. A fucking treat fit for a king his Cuban cock was, that was for sure... We passed his stinking and raunchy jock strap around, taking long hearty sniffs of it.

"Is that some fucked up legend too you bastards?" "Cooba" asked us, ranting and struggling to get untied. "Sniff a baseball player's jockstrap and become great baseball player's yourselves???"

When the jockstrap got to Dennis he tucked it into his pocket along with the baseball player's long navy blue socks.

He didn't comment on it, as he was more concerned at the moment with the way we had him tied down and what we were going to do to him next.

"M-my God, just look at this fu-fucked up position you guys got me in!!" the guy seethed. "F-fuck, what am I in for now you bastards??"

In response to his question we gathered around him at his most sensitive ticklish parts. Rodd and Angel took position at the baseball player's exposed very bushy very sweaty and stinking armpits. Dennis and Alex each stepped to one of the guy's bound feet and I stood over his stomach and crotch area. "Okay you guys, now," Dennis said and all at once we again started tickling the trapped baseball player.

"Ohhhhhrrrrrrrrrrrrrr!!!!! Ha, ha, ha, ha, ha, ha, ha, ha, ha, ha, ha, ha, ha, ha!!!!" "Cooba" cackled like crazy.

Rodd and Angel dug their fingertips deep into the guy's stinking moist armpits and really put the screws to them. Dennis and Alex trailed their fingertips over and over the bottoms of the baseball player's smelly feet, holding them by the ankles and leaning down to suck and slurp at his twitching toes. I relentlessly tickle tortured the guy's smooth washboard stomach area and dug a fingertip deep into his big belly button, swirling it around and around in there. I was drooling for his cock though, that was for more than sure. Beads of his piss and trails of pre cum were slithering from his wide sexy slit and sliding down the shaft of the beefy thing. "Cooba's" balls were the size of goose eggs, hanging nice and sweaty between his muscular legs and resting atop the padded table. He squirmed miserably atop that table, laughing and laughing his baldhead off.

"Ha, ha, ha, ha, ha, ha, ha, ha, ha, ha, ha, ha, ha, ha,

ha!!!!" he chortled loudly, his bound hands clenched into big fists.

When I could resist no longer I slowly leaned down and slathered the tip of my tongue over the crown of the baseball player's cock, getting a luscious sample of his great tasting cum and piss beads.

"Ha, ha, ha, ha, ha, ha, ha, ha, ha, ha, ha, ha, oooooooooooooooo, har, har, ha, ha, ha, ha, ha!!!!! Ohhhhhhrrrrrr g-gads, f-fucking guy man, h-he's goin' after my big cock!!!" the baseball player gasped, his head raised off the table, watching as no doubt it was the first time in his life that some guy had gone after his manhood.

"Fucking Chris man, I knew he would want to milk the fucking stud, I just fucking knew it," Angel said jovially, still tickling "Cooba's" armpit and watching as I slid my mouth slowly (oh so slowly) over "Cooba's" big beefy hardness. "We should have taken money bets on it. Even more than tickle torturing a guy there's nothing Chris loves more than milking the fuck out of them."

The baseball player's cock filled my mouth as I went down on it, slathering my tongue over and over every section of the thing as I went, my fingers still doing their dirty work and tickling the guy's stomach region. He bucked wildly on the table…

"Oh man, f-fucking guy is sucking my damned cock," the baseball player panted. "Ohhhhhh gads pl-please stop this!! I'm no faggot!! Ha, ha, ha, ha, ha, ha, ha, ha, ha, ha, ha, ha, ha!!!!"

"Cooba's cock tasted raw and was all raunchy and sexy with his musty scent. Fuck, after being cooped up in that smothering jock strap of his and more than three to four hours in the hot sun did I actually expect his cock to smell and taste good? Well, even raunchy smelling, the pitcher's cock tasted good. I slid my mouth further down the damn thing, sucking it heartily as I went. He was laughing and bucking and squirming in agony and ecstasy on that table all at once. When I finally had his cock all the way in my mouth my nose was pressed against his pubic bush. I sniffed it and slowly brought my mouth back up along his cock, my lips pressed hard against it as I went. I slowly slid my mouth back down and back up, slathering my tongue all over the great baseball player's shaft, loving the feel of it as I held it captive in my mouth.

"Ha, ha, ha, ha, ha, ha, ha, ha, ha, ha, ha, ha, ha, ha, ha, ha!!!!!! F-fucking guy, fucking guy is eating my damned beefy cock!!" the baseball player gasped. "An-and the rest of you, shit!!! S-stop tick-tickling me already!!! Ha, ha, ha, ha, ha, ha, ha, ha, ha, ha, ha!!!! Ohhhhrrrrrr, you fucker!!!!"

"Cooba's" big cock throbbed madly in my mouth, all hot and pulsing with a life of it's own. I knew it wouldn't be much longer before he was ready to shoot his load. I still continued to work it slowly with my mouth though, driving the poor pitcher into a frustrating and heated frenzy.

"Ohhhhhhrrrr shhhiiiitttttt," the baseball player gasped and bucked up and down on the table, his balls jiggling real nice against the tabletop.

As Rodd and Angel tickle tortured the guy's armpits and Dennis and Alex tickled his feet and sucked his toes I went on and on sucking his big meat stick, tickling his stomach at the same time.

"Ha, ha, ha, ha, ha, ha, ha, ha, ha, ha!!!! I-I am go-going to get all of you guys for this!!" the baseball player gasped. "Ohhhhhrrr fuck, oh, I-I'm goin' to fucking shoot my damned load you blasted mugs!! Un-unbelievable!!"

That was all I wanted to hear. I quickly stopped sucking the guy's cock. It twitched and bobbed between his legs uncontrollably, but he couldn't shoot his load.

"Ohhhhhrrrrr fuck, ohhhhrrr no, do-don't do this to me you fucking pervert!!" the tickle tortured baseball player swore up at me. "If, if you're going to suck my damned cock then at least let me shoot my load man!! Ha, ha, ha, ha, ha, ha, ha, ha, ha, ha, ha, ha, ha!!! Oh fuck man, what a real shitty thing to do to me!!"

"Ha, fucking Chris is going to make the guy wait to shoot his load," Angel said sadistically. "Oh well, we'll just have to tickle torture him some more to kill time."

"Cooba" screamed with laughter and his cock twitched longingly between his legs, longing to shoot that pent-up load of baseball player nut juice. He was sweating and stinking with it more than before atop that table and after another fifteen minutes of straight tickle torture we stopped. To us it was fifteen minutes, but to the tied up baseball player I was sure it felt more like hours.

"Oooooooooohhhhhhhhh, oh fuck, oh God, th-this was too mu-much guys," "Cooba" panted as we all looked around for bottles of water and champagne. "Re-real fucked up way to celebrate a winning game, but I'm glad I survived it. I wonder if any of my teammates have ever had something like this happen to them. Fuck, I wonder how many of them wanted to do it to me after they carried me in here after the game. Pl-please untie me and I can be on my way. No doubt my fiancée is wondering why I'm delayed."

"What are you talking about man?" Rodd asked the guy,

stepping behind his baldhead and squatting down. "That was just the warm-up. Fuck, you didn't even shoot your load yet." That said Rodd cupped his hands around the great "Cooba's" chin and kissed the top of his sweaty baldhead Bugs Bunny style, wet and sloppy and began tonguing it like crazy. "Bastards!! Let me out of here already!!" the baseball player roared in total panic. "And fuck man, stop licking my damned head!!! Of all things, shit!!"

We gave "Cooba" a few hearty drinks of mineral water and showered him with more champagne. He grunted and gurgled angrily as the champagne splashed over him. We made him chug down some of the champagne as well and by then I knew he had to piss like crazy. I wondered just how long he would be able to hold out. As Rodd licked the guy's baldhead I leaned down and sniffed his big mangy balls. They smelled as bad as his cock did but I tongued them heartily a few times anyway.

"F-fucking perverts, some fans you guys are!" "Cooba" swore angrily.

I hefted his balls up and was assaulted by the scent emanating from his sweaty and raw ass crack. Because his legs were widely splayed I had a great view of his raunchy hole. Oh God, I could not resist. Holding his big balls in my hand I slid my tongue into his clammy raunchy hole.

"Ohhhhrrr, f-fucking guy, goddamned pervert is licking my asshole!!" "Cooba" gasped loudly as Rodd still went on and on licking his baldhead. "Damn it all you guys, this is really twisted shit!! I wonder what the fuck Paul or Derek would do in a situation like this."

"Cooba's" big cock pulsed long and piss hard between his legs. I slithered my tongue deeper and deeper up into his hole. The guy hefted his butt cheeks off the table, giving me greater access to his stink hole.

"Ohhhhhhrrr fuck, ohhhhrrr, what a day this turned out to be!!" "Cooba" whimpered.

When Rodd and I stopped licking the baseball player's head and asshole we all once again took our respective positions at his ticklish sensitive parts. Break time was over for the poor trapped baseball player. All at once we resumed tickling his armpits, his feet and his stomach area. The sounds of "Cooba's" laughter and cackling filled and echoed through the locker room.

"Ha, ha, ha, ha, ha, ha, ha, ha, ha, ha, ha, ha!!!!" An-and here we fucking go again!!" the baseball player wailed despairingly.

Within five minutes the guy was in a lather and bucking and squirming miserably atop the table.

"Ha, ha, ha, ha, ha, ha, ha, ha, ha, ha, ha, ha, ha!!! Fu-fucking bastards!!" "Cooba" swore.

When he saw me leaning toward his big cock again he didn't say a word about it, he just seemed to get a hopeful look in his big eyes. Or was I imagining things? Was the great "Cooba" somehow secretly enjoying all this kinky attention we were heaping on him? Fuck man, that meat stick of his hadn't gone soft once during the whole ordeal. I slurped it greedily this time into my mouth and with my lips and tongue made love to it.

"Ohhhhh, fucking Chris loves my cock," "Cooba" said throatily. "Ha, ha, ha, ha, ha, ha, ha, ha, ha, ha, ha, ha, ha!!!! And the rest of you su-sure do love tickle torturing the fuck out

of me!! Ha, ha, ha, ha, ha, har, har, har, ha, ha, ha!!!!"
I slid my tongue around and around the guy's cock, poked my
tongue into his piss hole and was treated to tastes and
smidgens of his cum and piss. Man, he would shoot a load big
enough to choke a horse, when I decided to let him that is.

"Ohhhhrrr yeah, yeah man, yeah, of all the fucking
things, I-I'm getting close now you bastard!!" "Cooba said in
between hearty bouts of laughter.

I sucked him and sucked him and when he made the
mistake of saying that he was about to cum I again stopped,
taking his cock quickly out of my mouth.

"EEEEErrrhhhhhhh shiiiitttt, no, no!!! Ohhhhhrrrrr you
blasted mug!!!" the baseball player gasped almost pitifully, his
cock bobbing around like crazy, unable to spew that load of
man juices. "Fu-fuck man, th-this is awful!!"

I could just imagine how the guy felt as his cum no
doubt slithered back inside him, his balls churning not all that
pleasantly. God, his poor balls must have been aching at that
point. We tickled him harder and harder, really digging fingertips into his armpits, over and over his bare feet and his stomach area. If he weren't tied down to the table I'm sure he would
have flown off it when I jammed a finger into his stinking ass
hole.

"Ha, ha, ha, ha, ha, ha, ha, ha, ha, ha, ha, ha, ha!!!!! G-
get your damned finger outa my hole!!" the baseball player
rasped.

It was another twenty minutes before we stopped tickling
him again. By then the guy barely had any voice left. He was
heaving his laughter at that point, his muscular body straining
beautifully in the tight bondage and his big cock hard and

aching to shoot that load. He lay there trying to catch his breath as we stood around him, looking down at him in total awe, disbelief filling all of us at our luck at having snagged the great baseball player "Cooba...."

His cock was totally rock hard, attesting to the fact that somewhere deep inside the guy he secretly enjoyed what we had done to him thus far...

Rodd was again squatting behind the table and slathering his tongue all over the baseball player's baldhead.

"Damn, what is it with this guy and licking my bald-head?" "Cooba" complained.

To quiet him down I slurped his cock into my mouth...

"oooooooohhhhhhhhhrrrr, fucking guy just loves my big Cuban meat stick," the baseball player gasped breathlessly as I slid my mouth slowly down his hardness, obviously having found his voice again.

"Arrrrhhhhhhhhh yeah, got to admit, it feels fucking great guy," "Cooba" heaved as Rodd held his head in place by his chin, slathering his tongue all over the guy's bald sweaty head, even planting delicate kisses on his dome.

Goose bumps broke out all over the trussed up baseball player's magnificent body as Rodd and I feasted on him like crazy. Dennis and Alex leaned over the guy and slurped his big fleshy and meaty nipples into their mouths.

"Ohhhhhrrrrr, faggot fans you guys are!!" "Cooba" panted. "G-guys are makin' me fucking crazy with all this shit!!" Angel knelt at one of the baseball player's tied feet and suckled one of his big toes.

"Damn, fucking guys are really making me nuts now, eating my man tits, my cock, licking my damned baldy head and sucking my damned toes!!" "Cooba" said throatily. "Ohhhhrrrr, oh fuck, getting there now you cock hungry guy!!"

I grabbed the guy's balls in my hand and sucked the ballplayer like crazy. This time I would let him shoot his load. God knew he had earned the explosion after all.

"Ohhhhhhhhrrrrr yeahhhhh, fucking A!!!" "Cooba" gasped and pulled his head out of Rodd's grasp and looked down at me as he shot his big load into my mouth. "Ooooooooo, gads, fucking slob is eating my mess..."

"Oh yeah Chris, suck that load out of him, drain those big nuts of his!" Rodd said, pushing the great "Cooba's" head back down on the table and pouring champagne over him all over again.

"Ohhhhhrrrr yeah," "Cooba" gasped as his cum flooded and flooded my mouth.

I gulped down as much of it as I could, sucking and slurping on him at the same time. What I could not swallow dribbled out of the sides of my mouth. I squeezed his big nuts and that got yet another few globs of baseball player juice out of the guy. He shook and trembled in ecstasy on that table as we sucked him like crazy, even after he had finished shooting his big creamy load of hot spunk.

"Ooooooohhhhhhrrr fucking guys," he whispered as I sucked his semi hard and no doubt very sensitive cock deep into my mouth. "F-fuck man, I have to piss like a damned marine!"

With that I gave his balls another good squeeze and then the guy was pissing long hot and frothy into my mouth. Once again he raised his head to watch me.

"Ohhhhrrrr man, fucking guy is guzzling my piss," he gasped, thrusting his hips, forcing his cock further into my mouth.

"Cooba's" piss was hot and tasted rancid, but it was the greatest pitcher of all time's piss after all and I gladly guzzled down his long yellow frothy stream, sucking his cock at the same time, driving him crazier than crazy with it. He squirmed wildly on the table as we ate his man tits, sucked his now sensitive cock, licked his baldhead and sucked his toes. When I finally let the guy's cock slip from my mouth he was completely breathless. We stood around him as Dennis and Alex did the honors of untying the great baseball player. We were ready to run if he was going to decide to pay any of us back for what we'd just heaped on him...

"I hope you're not too pissed off with us Sir, Mr. "Cooba," Sir," Dennis said hopefully and nervously. "We just wanted to have some fun with you and show you how much we admire you."

With a sly looking grin on his face "Cooba" sat up on the table, leaning back on his elbows.

"Well, I suppose that I should be very pissed with you guys, I really should call the cops right now, but seeing as you went through all this trouble to land my ass I guess I should be sort of flattered," he said to us and we all cheered and whooped happily.

"You know, I brought a camera with me Mr. "Cooba", Sir, do you think we could get some pictures with you, in your uniform of course, and maybe a few autographs too?" Dennis asked the baseball player, sounding as desperate as possible.

"Cooba" looked at his rancid socks sticking out of Dennis' pocket and smirked for a second, no doubt thinking how the guy more than got a souvenir. I mean, how many of us out there can say that we have a pair of socks that were once worn by a famous baseball player?

"Let me get showered and into a clean uniform," "Cooba" replied, hopping down off the table and waiting a few seconds with his head down while the spinning faded from all the champagne. "Then we'll take some real winning pictures."

We clapped him on the back and playfully swatted his great ass ala baseball player style as he walked toward the shower room…

A little while later we were outside the locker room. "Cooba" had donned a fresh uniform after a nice warm sudsy shower. He was in his white pinstripes complete with his cap and a fresh pair of those knee length navy blue socks of his that we love seeing him in. He was wearing sneakers rather than cleats now, seeing as he was just posing for pictures. We took a few shots of him standing with Dennis, seeing as it was Dennis who had gotten us the tickets for the game. We took some of him standing with all of us, courtesy of the fact that Dennis' camera had a built-in timer. With his camera set up on a fence facing us Dennis and the rest of us posed for the last few shots with the great baseball player.

"Hey, for the last few lets do it right, I mean really right," Dennis said, hooking a hand around "Cooba's" arm. "Let's get the hero of today's game up on our shoulders, just like his teammates did earlier."

"Cooba" grinned from ear to ear as we hoisted him off the ground and to our shoulders. We all smiled real big as the camera clicked. Dennis held "Cooba's" socked ankle close and tight.

"Okay you guys, looks like that's it," "Cooba" said. "This was some experience I must say. Twisted but interesting at the same time, know what I mean? I better be on my way now though so if you'll just put me down now..."

As the great baseball player spoke we all turned around in unison and carried him back into the locker room, slowly, the camera clicking as we lugged him...

"H-hey, put me down you guys," "Cooba" squabbled angrily now. "Come on now, you've had more than your sadistic fun with me! Gads, put me down already!!"

His arms flailed uselessly out at his sides and there wasn't all that much that he could do as he was perilously balanced up there on our shoulders. He ranted angrily as we carted him back into the locker room; no doubt he knew what we had in mind...

A few minutes later the sound of insane laughter filled the locker room as we again had the great "Cooba" all tied up and tickle tortured the fuck out of him...

Mr. Kujman's Device

Author's Note:

This story was inspired by a devilish device called the "Laff-o-matic" which was brought to my attention by my Internet buddy "The Executive Tickler" and was invented by his Internet buddy Mr. Kujman. Special and heartfelt thanks go out to Mr. Kujman for allowing me to star his tickle torture device in my story and to have some liberties of my own with it. Thank you also to Mr. Kujman for allowing me to star him as the wicked but campy inventor in my story… Also, special thanks go out to my good buddy Rick, for the inspiration where the manicure buffers as tickle torture devices are concerned…
Happy Reading to all…

      I could not believe it when I was given the news by the top partner in the law firm that I work for. We had landed a really big client, Mr. Lewis Kujman, I was told was his name, he was an inventor of sorts, and I had been selected as the lawyer to patent his latest invention, or his device as he wanted it called. When Mr. Gordon Richards came into my office that Monday afternoon to tell me the greater than great news I was ecstatic. According to what Richards told me Mr. Kujman was the creator of various exercise machines for some world famous health clubs, he had invented a new wave of copier and fax machines for some big corporate companies and he was even responsible, very discreetly for inventing some new household items to make homeowners lives a bit easier. And to add to his creative résumé he had also invented some party devices, as they were supposedly called. Seeing as my wife and I had just become homeowners ourselves I figured I could look into some of Mr. Kujman's inventions and creations for us. Actually, little did I know just how very intimately I would come to know one of the inventor's creations. I imagined that the man had to be beyond rich, seeing as he had invented devices for more than just one walk of life. Exercise machines, office equipment, household items and even party devices, and yet I had never heard of the man. Now, according to the top partner in my firm, Mr. Gordon Richards, Mr. Kujman had invented a device that would be a big splash at parties of all kinds. He said it was called "The O-matic" and he had hired our firm to patent it, me being the patent lawyer to draw up all the legal documents and paperwork and to bill the client. From what Mr. Richards told me as he sat in my office with me a nice hefty commission was in store for me where this deal was concerned. After Mr. Richards left my office I smiled from ear to ear and picked up the phone to call my wife with the great news. As I spoke to her I leaned back in my chair, propped my wingtip shoed feet up on my desk and visions of dollar signs danced before me...

My name is Byron Merrick; I'm thirty years old, a corporate lawyer with a firm named "Richards, Gage, and Sommers", located in good old New York City. I'm originally from Dallas Texas, which would explain my sort of leftover accent. I'm hoping to make partner within the firm in a year or two. I've been with the firm now for a tad more than three years. I have short cut black hair, dark blue eyes and stand five feet ten inches tall on my size ten and a half socked feet. (Good Lord, why'd I mention my big ol' socked feet for? Since my meeting and encounter with Mr. Kujman just mentioning my size ten and a half's gets me nearly insane, just like when I said that I had put my feet up on my desk when I called my wife, but more on that soon I promise, good laws yes!) My body is rock hard, firm and better than well-muscled from the daily workouts that I put and punish myself through at the gym four times a week after work and once on the weekends on Sunday afternoons. I've been married for four years at this point to my beautiful wife. Her name is Carolyn. We have no children yet, but since we now own a house we figure that within a couple of years we will start a family... Good Lord, I wonder how my children would like hearing someday about what Mr. Lewis Kujman subjected their dad to on that fateful day...

It was a hot, humid and sticky day in Manhattan when my client Mr. Kujman had decided that he would bring me to his large house on Long Island to see the device, the O-matic as he called it, that he was paying the firm to patent. I had met him that past Monday and over lunch in a ritzy, glitzy and very costly restaurant we had set up the appointment. The top partner in our firm, Gordon Richards, again, brought our newest client to my office personally. He stood a little shorter than me with reddish wavy hair and small beady looking eyes behind thick coke bottle bottom glasses. When I shook hands with Mr. Kujman he held tight to my palm and really squeezed it hard, seeming to drink in the sight of me at the same time. I almost got the feeling that I was being devoured in his stare. My mother had taught me that a person with a strong gripped handshake was a sincere person. If that were so then why did the short hairs on the back of my neck gristle and seem to stand on end when Mr. Kujman pumped my hand and told me how wonderful and exciting it was to meet me? Exciting to meet me? What the hell was so exciting about me I wondered at his choice of words? Richards said that his secretary had secured lunch reservations for our distinguished client and me at a nearby and very well known restaurant, unless Mr. Kujman had other ideas for lunch that day. Man, could Richards kiss ass when it came to the clients of our firm. Mr. Kujman said that any restaurant would be superb, still drinking in the sight of me it seemed and still holding tight to my hand as he pumped it and we spoke with Mr. Richards. For a fleeting moment I got the distinct feeling that I was being sized up for something. My word, how right I was and how sorry I would be. Mr. Kujman looked like a typical inventor, by typical I mean he had an eccentric look about him, I say that in a good way. I'm of the belief that inventors are an eccentric breed, separate from the rest of us, artists if you would, bohemian. He sat across from me in the restaurant wearing a seer sucker suit, white shirt with a blue tie, very old fashioned gentlemanly looking. What I hadn't mentioned earlier was that he sported a thinly trimmed red mustache, slightly curled up at the sides. If I didn't know better I would swear that it was one of those thin mustaches that the villains in the old time silent movies used to have. Actually, that villainous looking mustache would be very fitting very soon for the scene that he had in mind for me and him, a scene that I would unwittingly be starring in. I was clad in a navy blue pin-striped suit with a white shirt and burgundy tie. When he smiled at me his eyes seemed to bug out through his thick glasses, making it seem he was really devouring me with his stare. I decided that it was all my imagination. After we ordered a couple of drinks to sip before lunch I explained to Mr. Lewis Kujman that I needed to see the device before I could issue him a patent license for it, stating kindly that it was the law after all. With a big smile on his face he raised his glass to his moist looking lips and said, "Of course Mr. Merrick, I understand completely. I've been through this sort of thing with other firms and it was quite a feat even then let me tell you." He sipped his drink a couple of times and for whatever the reason I found that my feet (feat???) were sweating in my socks at that moment.

"I could of course provide a company car to bring me to your place of residence to see the device," I began to say. "I'll bring all the necessary paperwork, a camera..."

"Hogwash!! I will drive you there myself, it will be my pleasure," the inventor said and sipped his drink again, grinning it seemed from ear to ear. "But please do have the necessary paperwork and a camera."

"Of course," I said, sounding unsure, seeing as the client never drove a member of our firm anywhere, it was always the other way around.

Hogwash? Had he actually said hogwash? Good Lord, the last time I heard that expression was way back in my junior high school days when the assistant principal had said it. But then again, I always said "Good Laws", an expression I picked up from a classic Stephen King story way back.

But if this was what the client wanted this was what the client got... I would allow him to drive me to his place of residence; of course I would let Mr. Richards know about this strange turn of events.

We decided that I would go with him to his place of residence that Wednesday morning. I would get some pictures of the device for my files, have him sign the necessary and legal documents and then issue him a patent for his latest invention. When I confirmed the address of his home he again insisted on driving me there himself, stating that he would be glad to pick me up at my office and then drive me back after we were done with the business at hand. Seeing as he was the client I didn't try to counter his offer again. It seemed that he was hell bent on driving me there, actually it seemed that he was hell bent on getting me there himself. I also had to wonder why a man of his prestige and position didn't have a chauffeur to drive us to his place of residence. This whole thing seemed strange from the beginning I have to say and sadly I didn't pay attention to my lawyerly instincts. We agreed that he would pick me up in front of the office building around 9:30 AM that coming Wednesday. I figured I would bring a digital camera (Good laws, mistake, very big mistake bud)... For the rest of our lunch engagement Mr. Lewis Kujman and I made general small talk. He asked if I were married, I told him that I was and showed him a picture that I keep in my wallet of my wife and myself. He looked at the picture intently, the way he had looked at me earlier upon our meeting each other, as if he were drinking in the picture of my wife and me. After I put the picture away he told me how he had never married or settled down with a partner, citing the fact that he'd never met the right person. I kindly told him that there was someone out there for everyone, but then figured that I'd better mind my business. He mumbled something about being married to his work. With a sad looking smirk on his face he raised his glass, sipped his drink and asked if I had any children at this point... I had to wonder a bit as his over curiosity about my personal life, but then again, he was the client... To soften the somewhat tense atmosphere I told Mr. Kujman how I had been told that he had invented devices that could be big splashes at parties, adding how I might be interested in some of them, seeing as my wife and I had just recently become home owners. The inventor was delighted at my interest in his work and his eyes seemed to bug out again behind his thick glasses, good laws that were creepy. He sipped his drink noisily while again seeming to drink in the sight of me... I quickly added how my wife and I would more than likely also be interested in some of the household items he had invented...

At 9:30 AM on the overly hot and humid Wednesday that Mr. Kujman and I had agreed upon I was waiting for him outside the office building that I work in. That day I was clad in a plain lightweight dark blue suit, a crisp white shirt and a dark green silk necktie, specially knotted by my wife that morning for good luck. Every time my wife knots my tie for me I get a hard on. I was sweating like crazy as I stood there waiting for the inventor, attaché case in hand. People standing outside the building were already taking their first cigarette break of the day. At 9:35 AM Mr. Kujman pulled up in his car and I could not believe what I was seeing as his car was a worn looking Chevy with the windows all rolled down. I instantly realized that he had no air conditioning in his car.

"Good morning Mr. Merrick," Mr. Kujman called out to me, smiling from ear to ear. "How are you today my good man?"

"Doing well thanks, good morning to you too Mr. Kujman," I replied in my baritone sounding voice, my Texas accent sliding in there, seeing as I was miffed as hell at this turn of events where the client's car was concerned. (Whenever I'm irritated or angry over something my accent always sneaks up on me...my wife teases and razzes me about it all the time...)

If you think I was miffed over this turn of events just wait till after I saw Mr. Kujman's device bud...

"Sadly the air conditioning in my car seems to have chosen today of all days to quit one me," he said to me as I climbed somewhat reluctantly into the passenger seat, resting my attaché case on my lap.

I couldn't help noticing the cigarette puffing people snickering and making snide remarks about the well-dressed handsome lawyer climbing into the crappy and beat-up looking jalopy-like car. The leather seat seemed to literally absorb me as I sank into it after getting the car door closed.

"We could uh, still take a company car," I suggested, my Texas accent sliding in again as I took a long white cloth handkerchief from my suit jacket pocket and mopped my forehead. "I could arrange for a car instantly Mr. Kujman. I wouldn't even mind driving, wouldn't mind at all."

"Nonsense, I'm glad to drive," he said as I settled as best I could into the sticky seat, the heat in the car torturous to say the least. "Loosen your tie; unbutton your top shirt button. I don't stand on formality after all. And besides, having that tie choking you is no doubt making the heat feel even worse. Once we're on the highway with the breeze blowing you'll be fine Mr. Merrick, you'll see..."

"Uh, yes Sir," I said sheepishly, sounding Texan as hell as he pulled out into the traffic.

As I pulled my tie down I thought of my wife gingerly making the knot in it for me that morning, her lips grazing the back of my neck as she stood behind me at the mirror as she slowly fashioned the knot...

"Where are you originally from Mr. Merrick?" the inventor asked me, stealing a grin at me as I pulled my tie further down. "Texas, Dallas Texas," I replied as the heat in the car cooked me.

"Ah, a cowboy then," Mr. Kujman mused.

There was no breeze when we got on the highway, seeing as the early morning rush hour traffic was backed up nearly bumper to bumper... The really strange thing that I noticed though, but didn't mention was the fact that Mr. Kujman didn't seem to be sweating at all in the intense heat of the car...

"Did you bring all the necessary paperwork and a camera?" he asked me as he drove slowly on the highway.

"Got it all right here Sir," I replied, patting the top of my attaché case, then reaching up and unbuttoning my top shirt button.

"Good, good," the inventor said and patted my thigh. (I stifled a gulp at his touch as his hand actually felt cold as ice through my suit pants.)

I wished that I could take my suit jacket off but the way I was wedged in the car made that impossible… The ride from my office building in Manhattan to Long Island should take, the most, forty minutes. With the traffic that we had encountered it took a little more than an hour. The heat made it seem like double that time. It was ten fifty five AM when I stepped out of Mr. Kujman's car, holding tight to the handle of my attaché case with my sweaty palm. I gingerly closed the car door when in reality what I wanted to do was slam it angrily. The seat of my suit pants were literally stuck to me, my armpits felt all moist and sweaty and my feet felt like they were swollen to twice their size in my thin navy blue socks and black shiny lace-up wingtips. (Oh Good Laws, and there I go again mentioning my poor feet again. And this time I even made mention of my poor socks. Gads!! You'll see what I mean when I say "my poor socks" very soon.) It had to be at least ninety five degrees that day with more than a hundred percent humidity. I mopped my forehead again with my handkerchief, and as I was doing so I noticed that Mr. Kujman was still sitting in the car. I quickly pocketed my handkerchief, gulped hard and dashed over to his door. Seeing as he was the client he expected that I should open the car door for him. I did as the client expected.
"Ah, thank you, thank you Mr. Merrick," he said as he stepped out of the car. "Well, here we are then, as they say."
"Yes Sir," I replied, closing the car door and took in the sight of his immense house. "Here we are."

The house was enormous, mansion-like actually, situated by itself on a long stretch of property, prime Long Island real estate to be exact. I saw neatly trimmed hedges, large trees and beautiful rose bushes as Mr. Kujman led the way to the front door, holding my arm as we walked...

"The "O-matic is in the basement of the house," Mr. Kujman said as he let go of my arm, took a keychain from his pocket and with one of many keys on it opened the front door. "The basement is actually where I do all my inventing and cre-ating of my numerous devices. I find it to be quite pleasant and relaxing down there."

"I understand," I replied.

I almost expected to see a servant or butler of some kind open the door for us, but none was in attendance it seemed. Actually, I got the feeling that it was just Mr. Kujman and I there and with that reality setting in a chill seemed to climb up my spine and settle on the back of my neck. Once again I felt the short hairs on the back of my neck gristle and once again I stupidly ignored it. Being a lawyer I should have known to pay attention to that feeling.

"The basement is this way," Mr. Kujman stated, pointing the way toward a large kitchen as I took in the surroundings of his enormous house as we walked through the living room.

"Yes, the basement, where you do all your inventing," I said.

The inside of the house felt cool, but I could tell that the air conditioning was not on. For whatever the reason I got the strangest feeling that Mr. Kujman wanted me sweating. My wingtips sunk into a plush dark beige carpet in the state of the art living room. As Mr. Kujman led the way to the basement I saw expensive works of art adorning the walls of the immense living room, a modern sectional style couch aligned one wall and a large love seat faced it from the other wall. A large glass coffee table dominated the center of the fancy living room and huge vases of fresh flowers were set atop the two matching end tables. The inventor was more than well off, that was for sure. I had been right about that. I guessed that he was paid well for his creations. It must be great to make money with the stuff you invent I thought. As we made our way through the living room I again mopped my forehead with my handkerchief. If Mr. Kujman noticed my discomfort from the heat, even in the house, he made no mention of it, nor did he apologize for it. I had to wonder why a man who had a house like this one would drive such a cheesy car and one where the air conditioning in it decides to quit on one of the hottest days of the year at that. I also wondered how many servants the inventor employed, seeing as there was no way that he could keep this house looking the way it did on his own. And gads, where were those servants today? Once again I got the distinct feeling that it was just Mr. Kujman and I in the house that day, and I also got the feeling that that was just the way he wanted it. We passed quickly through one of the largest kitchens I had ever seen, which led to the basement, to hell actually, although I didn't know that at the time. I choked on and stifled an angry grunt when I happened to glance out one of the kitchen windows. In a carport outside the house I saw a luxury-sized black Cadillac. It looked brand new and I got the distinct feeling that the air-conditioning in it would work perfectly, if I checked that is. It was a limousine-like car actually; the kind a chauffeur or some other kind of house servant would drive. My anger boiled up in me even more when I realized that the inventor himself could have sent a car for me, a comfortable car at that. Instead I was cooked and made to sweat to the point of more than discomfort in a cheesy and old rundown jalopy so to speak, but why? My anger and confusion caused me to sweat even more. I got the feeling that as we passed by that window that Mr. Kujman wanted me to see that car out there in the carport. Holding my attaché case tight in my sweaty palm I followed Mr. Kujman down the basement stairs. The basement was cool at least, as most basements are, even during the hottest summer days. Like the main floor of the house the basement was immense, what most people would call "totally finished."

"I have the device in the workshop part of the basement, as I like to call it," Mr. Kujman said as we walked through the basement toward a closed door.

The inventor stopped at the closed door and again took out his keychain.

"I keep it under wraps so to speak," he said, glancing back at me with a look of pure glee in his eyes, his eyes seeming to enlarge under his thick glasses. "Until I have an invention patented I don't like for anyone to see it for fear of having my idea stolen and possibly replicated. I hope that makes sense to you Mr. Merrick."

"That it does Mr. Kujman," I said, giving the knot in my pulled down tie a twist, smiling at the client. "And very good thinking on your part I might add Sir."

He turned back and slid the key into the lock on the door to the room he called his workshop.

"I'm so excited that it's unbelievable," he said, his hand almost shaking as he turned the key. "Whenever I'm about to show a new invention to someone for the first time I become like an anxious child."

I pursed my lips in a smile as he looked back at me again, the door to the workshop slightly ajar, but not ajar enough to see what was inside just yet. This time it was obvious that he was looking at me in a hungered and lustful way. I felt a chill creep up my spine but I still maintained my professional aura.

"Tell me Mr. Merrick, would you humor an eccentric inventor?" Mr. Kujman asked me, almost sweating now himself, but not quite half as much as he had sweated me in his car.

It still amazed me that he didn't seem to be sweating all that much, the heat being as intense as it was that day...

"Uh, humor you?" I asked him, grinning now, my pearly white teeth showing. "How would you like for me to humor you Sir?"

"Well, I don't want you to see my invention until you're in the workshop," he said to me. "I want you to see it when you are standing directly in front of it and not before. Would you mind if I blindfolded you, just until we're in the workshop?"

"I, uh," I began to say.

"Your white cloth handkerchief would do perfectly for that purpose," he said, pointing at my suit jacket pocket, obviously not intending to take "no" for an answer. "It's long enough to serve as a blindfold. I'll guide you in, I won't let you trip or bump into anything at all. I give you my word on that Mr. Merrick."

"Uh, that sure is a strange request Mr. Kujman," I said, smiling sheepishly now, but finding myself reaching into my suit jacket pocket for my slightly sweat sopped handkerchief. "But I don't see why not, no pun intended."

As I spoke I noticed that my Texas accent was sliding in. Obviously I was more than slightly taken aback by Mr. Kujman's request. Blindfold me???

"Ah, thank you, thank you Mr. Merrick," the inventor said, taking my monogrammed handkerchief from me and quickly stepping behind me. "This is truly a wonderful day for me. You're going to be the first person to see my latest invention. So I suppose it's sufficed to say that it's a wonderful day for you too."

"Yes Sir, a wonderful day," I said in my Texas accent as he was now standing behind me.

I stood there gripping my attaché case handle real tight as Mr. Kujman stretched my handkerchief out real long and then tied it over my eyes, slowly it seemed, as if he was thoroughly enjoying this moment, as if in ecstasy. For the briefest of seconds I could have sworn that I felt his fingertips trail along the back of my neck, just above my shirt collar, an area that my wife seems to lust after a lot of the time. Once again the short hairs back there gristled. Just like in his car his fingers felt cold and icy. I wondered how that could be, seeing as it was hot as all hell that day. As he knotted the handkerchief against the back of my head I recalled (for whatever the reason) that my wife had bought me the over-sized monogrammed handkerchiefs. I couldn't recall if they had been a birthday gift or perhaps an anniversary gift. I wondered if she ever thought for a second that her handsome husband would wind up blindfolded with one of them though. I knew she would get a good laugh out of it when I told her that night.

"Okay then, can you see anything?" the inventor asked me and I heard the door to the workshop pushed open now.

"Not a thing Mr. Kujman," I replied, sounding slightly nervous.

The scent of sweat on my handkerchief seeped into my

nostrils seeing as the inventor had tied it close down to my nose, insuring that I would have to keep my eyes closed under the white cloth.

"Then lets go on in," he said to me and once again standing behind me he grabbed both my upper arms this time. Per his promise he guided me slowly into the room he called the workshop, the room that I would come to call hell. Squeezing my arms tight as he led me into the room he didn't let me trip or bump into anything either. His hands squeezing my upper arms actually felt like two claws bud and again the short hairs on the back of my neck gristled. With that danged thin and curled mustache of his making him look like a villain from an old-time movie I felt like I was the captured hero of sorts, when in reality I was, I just didn't know it yet.
"Okay, right here is very good," Mr. Kujman said; positioning me in the spot he wanted me standing in for the unveiling so to speak. "Okay, oh, this is an exciting moment in an exciting day Mr. Merrick."

"Yes Sir, it is at that," I replied, feeling real stupid and silly standing there with my eyes covered.

"Let me take that for you," Mr. Kujman said and I felt myself being relieved of my attaché case.

I heard it placed on the floor nearby.

"May I see now Mr. Kujman?" I asked the inventor, reaching up to take the blindfold off.

"No, no, not yet Mr. Merrick," he said rather sternly. "I will take the blindfold off you if you don't mind."

"No Sir, I don't mind at all," I lied with a grin.

"Okay then, the moment has arrived," Mr. Kujman said and I felt him standing beside me then.

He placed his fingers on the knot in the blindfold.

"Please count slowly to three Mr. Merrick," he said as I tugged nervously at my tie.

"Uh, sure thing Sir," I said. "One, two..."

"Slowly Mr. Merrick, slowly," the eccentric inventor said.

Still grinning I thought what a kick my office buddies would get when they heard about me being blindfolded by a wacky client, but it would be me who got the bigger kick when I received my commission check.

"Uh, three..." I said a few seconds later.

Mr. Kujman whipped the blindfold off me, handing my handkerchief back to me...

As I took in the sight of the device in front of me I neatly folded up my handkerchief and slipped it back into my suit jacket pocket.

"Well uh, I say, what do we have here?" I asked the inventor, glancing at him and smiling.

The O-matic device, as Mr. Kujman called it consisted of various parts, devices, and apparatus's all very cleverly put together. As my eyes adjusted back to the light I took in the sight of it, my eyes roaming slowly over it I made observations about what those various parts were... At the topmost part of it on a raised platform a few feet off the floor the thing began with what looked like a combination of a long cushioned dentists/barbers chair. On the sides and along the leg-rest section of the chair I saw long leather heavy-duty straps, no doubt used to keep the party participant secure in the device. At the end of the long leg-rest I saw a square shaped piece of thick wood, sanded smooth on the edges and it had a perfectly round hole, cut semi-large directly in the center of it. I duly noted that the square piece of wood was mounted on tracks along the leg-rest. I guessed that this was to accommodate taller and shorter party participants who wanted to have some fun in the O-matic. Although Mr. Kujman still hadn't told me exactly what the "fun" would consist of for participants of the device. I also noted how the square piece of wood with the semi-large hole in it was actually two pieces of wood slid together. The top portion could be removed and slid down over the bottom portion. I had to wonder at the necessity for that. Mounted on a small table on the opposite side of the piece of wood with the hole in it I saw a very strange looking device indeed. It was round and oval in shape, sort of the shape of a giant Easter egg. It was beige in color. Buttons and knobs adorned the thing on both sides and protruding from the front of it were two long plastic stick-like instruments. On the ends of the instruments were little claws (or hooks if you would) that looked like "holders" for other instruments to be attached to. As I continued taking in the sight of the O-matic I ran a hand over it in sections. Mr. Kujman, standing a few short feet away from me, watching intently as I did the necessary inspection did not know that visions of those dollar signs were again dancing before my eyes as I ran a hand over his machine, device if you would.

"Now you understand why I wanted you blindfolded when I brought you in here, yes Mr. Merrick?" he asked me.

"I-I suppose so Mr. Kujman," I replied, my Texas accent sliding in again, but me not knowing exactly why. "Laws yes..."

"What do you think of it?" he asked me as I gripped a lever that was set up next to the device.

"Interesting looking device," I responded, let go of the lever and put my best lawyerly grin on for him as I glanced back at the inventor.

Gads, I was still trying to figure out exactly what the O-matic did. It looked like a bunch of stuff all thrown together very haphazardly. This was an invention by the same man who had invented world-famous devices? No way! I walked alongside the long chair, past the lever, taking in the sight of the long instruments on the sides of it. They were each smaller versions of the egg shaped devices in the front of it. Buttons and knobs adorned the smaller egg shaped devices as well and like the big one in front of the machine they had little claws (hooks) protruding from the fronts of them. I stepped away from the device and rocked back and forth on my wingtip heels, smiling my lawyerly smile.

"Okay, I, uh, I've seen it," I said, holding up my hands, palms flat out. "But what I really need now is to see what it does Mr. Kujman."

"Well now, this is a surprise, I hadn't planned on a demonstration Mr. Merrick," the inventor stated, sounding sorrowful. "I would need for someone to be here so that I could have them sit in the device while it was being demonstrated. If you had told me that you wanted a demonstration I would have had a friend or perhaps an associate who could..."

I quickly waved one of my hands back and forth, stopping him in mid sentence.

"Mr. Merrick?" he asked me.

"There is no need to have anyone come for a demonstration Mr. Kujman," I said, pointing a finger at myself. "I'm here after all."

"Oh dear, I couldn't," the inventor said. "I mean its trouble enough that you came here in my un-air-conditioned car, only because it's my driver's day off, but to have to do the demonstration too?"

"I'll consider it part of the job Sir," I said. "I'll sit in the device, you can demonstrate the mechanics and just what it does and then afterwards I'll get some pictures of it and then I'll have you sign the necessary papers and legal documents."

He seemed to mull it over for more than a few seconds, glancing back and forth at me and his machine, at me and his machine, at me and his machine. What I didn't know at that moment was that I had played right into his clutches, that I had done just what he'd hoped I would do, namely volunteer to sit in the danged device.

"Alright then Mr. Merrick, I agree with you, I don't see why not," he said happily.

I clapped my hands together, shucked off my suit jacket and said "Lets do it" sounding real corporate and eager. Gads!! I had just signed my own torture warrant and I didn't even know it. I hung my suit jacket on the back of the long combination dentists/barbers chair and then stood next to the seat. I awaited the inventor's instructions.

"Just climb up in there, stretch your legs out in the legrests and I'll get you secured in," Mr. Kujman said, giving one of my upper arms a gentle squeeze. "You will find that seat and the position you'll be in to be most comfortable Mr. Merrick."

"Uh, yeah sure," I said, tugging nervously on my tie
again, wondering if this was such a good idea after all.
I didn't like the sound of the words "secured in" all that much…
But it was too late to back out now…

I gripped the arm of the chair, hoisted myself up and sat
down in it, stretching my legs out in front of me in the long leg-
rests, per Mr. Kujman's instructions…

"Comfortable?" the inventor asked me, standing next to
my feet, grabbing my ankles and getting my feet and legs situated perfectly straight in the leg-rests.

"Actually, yeah, I am," I replied, another chill crawling up
my back and settling at the back of my neck as the inventor
handled my socked ankles. "Very comfortable. I may even buy
a chair like this for my office."

"Good, good, then we're off to a proper demonstration,"
Mr. Kujman said, stepping over to my upper body area.

He took hold of one of the heavy-duty straps and before
I could react or even protest he pulled it tight over my upper
body, literally pinning me to the chair, securing my muscular
arms at my sides, making them totally useless actually.

"Uh, Mr. Kujman?" I asked, sounding nervous, my Texas
accent sliding in and very pronounced now.

"Nothing to worry about Mr. Merrick, it's all part of the
demonstration that you volunteered for," he said and quickly
pulled a second strap over me, a few inches under the first
one, securing it tight around my upper body.

"Yes well, but when I saw the straps Sir I just figured
that they would be applied over the torso, not over the arms as

well," I said stupidly.

"Wrong," Mr. Kujman said with a grin, his beady eyes bugging out big and wide under his thick glasses. "Wrong." (Oh God, what had I gotten myself into here???)

He quickly yanked a third strap over me around my waistline area, thus totally securing my upper body to the chair. I couldn't help but notice how wrinkled my crisp white shirt was going to be and my silk tie as well.

Needless to say I could not move an inch...

"Uh, Mr. Kujman," I said again. "There really is no need to secure me in so tightly. I mean, just a simple demonstration would suffice and..."

"Ah no Merrick, I want this to be a very proper demonstration," the inventor said, almost with passion in his voice. "If you are going to grant me a patent then you need to see my device do exactly what it's meant to do... And even if you hadn't so kindly volunteered for this someone else assisting me would have been strapped in just as you are now. It's part of the procedure after all."

"Alright, I suppose you've got a point there Sir," I said, trying to sound like a combination businessman and lawyer at the same time. "As we say at the firm you are the client."

"That I am," the inventor said.

He smiled at me from ear to ear, almost fiendishly, and again that chill crept up my spine and settled on the back of my neck... With that thin and curled mustache of his he really did look like one of those wacky and campy villains from an old fashioned silent movie...

"Okay, very good, very, very good, it's going very well so far I would say," Mr. Kujman said, stepping quickly to the foot of the device behind the square piece of wood with the semi-large hole cut in it.

He moved the piece of wood on its tracks right up to the bottoms of my wingtips. Then, I watched with my eyes wide open in horror as he lifted my feet by the ankles and slid them through the semi-large hole. I gulped hard, starting to figure out just what the devilish device was for...God Almighty!!! Before I could even think to yank my feet out of the hole Mr. Kujman slid the topmost part of the piece of wood down over the tops of my feet, securing them in, literally trapping them. The sound of that piece of wood sliding down and locking my feet within the center in that hole was nearly maddening. I gulped hard again. My size ten and a half's were trapped in the stocks-like looking piece of wood. Mr. Kujman pulled the piece of wood back toward himself a few scant inches, insuring that my legs stayed long and stretched out. I could not move my legs at this point; at best all I could do was wiggle my toes within my socks and shoes.

"Uh, Mr. Kujman," I began again, my voice trembling this time, my lips quivering. "Uh, I would say that this demonstration was sufficient. If you would be so kind now to release me I'll start the necessary paperwork and..."

"But the demonstration has hardly begun at all," the inventor said and secured straps around my legs, lashing them to the leg-rests they were resting in. "I haven't even turned the device on yet."

"That's uh, that's what I'm afraid of Sir," I said softly, looking down at my poor feet trapped in the hole, my Texas accent really paramount now.

I took note of how his hands seemed to be trembling and a look of sheer ecstasy had come over his face as he did his work.

"Okay, that part of the demonstration is done," he said, looking me over as I looked at him with eyes filled with horror.

"Mr. Kujman," I whispered as he stepped to the foot of the machine again and squatted down at the egg shaped device.

He got the device situated directly at the bottoms of my feet and then pulled it back a few feet. The hooks (claws) on the end of the thing seemed to be mocking me. I watched as the inventor stepped to a cabinet, opened it and took out two long sticks, (I gulped hard, the hardest yet) two long sticks with feathers attached to the end of each of them.

"Oh fuck," I squeaked in outright horror now, knowing all too well at that point just what the device was for.

Mr. Kujman again squatted at the egg shaped device and attached the sticks with feathers on them to the ends of the hooks. They slipped in perfectly.

"Getting the idea?" he asked me, sounding totally fiendish now.

"Unfortunately for me I am," I said, not thinking for a second that he would do what he was about to do next.

Standing behind the piece of wood that my feet were encased in and sticking out of I watched as the inventor started unlacing my wingtips.

"H-hey, oh good laws, wh-what are you doing?" I stammered miserably. "Ah shit Mr. Kujman, don't take my shoes off me, please Sir!!"

With my lips pursed in a mixture of anger and fear I watched as my pleas were ignored and the inventor slowly unlaced my wingtips some more, finally sliding them off me, starting at the heel, sort of the way a proper shoe salesman would do it...

I grimaced miserably watching him put my shoes one at a time over his nose and mouth, inhaling my sweaty foot scent pretty heartily...

"Ah geez Mr. Kujman, oh good laws no, don't be sniffing my shoes now," I said in a huff, seeing my shoes off my feet and in his hands to be something that should not be part of a business deal. "You should hear how my wife complains about how my big ol' feet smell at the end of the day when I get home and take my danged shoes off."

"I would love to hear it," he mused, grinning, and placed my shoes on the floor after sniffing the inside of them a few more times.

(I asked myself again just what the fuck I had gotten myself into here...)

As he squatted to put my shoes down he stopped to sniff at my size ten and a half socked feet as they stuck out of the hole in the square piece of wood... I grimaced miserably again...

"Ah man, sniffing my socked feet too?" I asked him in disbelief as he took long hearty sniffs at my socks on my feet. "What is this all about Mr. Kujman???"

With my eyes still opened wide in disbelief I watched as the inventor sniffed and smelled the gold section of my Gold Toe brand socks, that area always being the smelliest it seemed. But then, horror of all horrors combined, I watched helplessly as the inventor slowly started sliding my thin navy blue nylon socks off my feet, starting at the smelly (gold) toes section.

"Oh God no, no!!! D-don't take my socks off me Mr. Kujman!!! Oh good laws, what is this???" I grumbled loud and miserably, struggling now to free myself from the device, but that of course was impossible, seeing as the straps securing me were too tight.

With my eyes now wide open in total and maddening terror I watched as my feet were slowly relieved of my moist and smelly socks. The inventor had them by the very smelliest section, as I said, the gold of the toe section. You guys out there who wear Gold Toe brand socks more than likely know that when it comes to those socks stinking and reeking, that it's the gold of the toe section that stinks the most, for whatever the reason. I think that whoever created those socks had that in mind, seeing as he must have been some kind of foot and sock fetishist himself. Mr. Kujman was bunching my socks up in his hand as he slowly slid them off me.

"Oh gads, oh Gods no," I whimpered, wriggling my toes in the socks while they were still halfway on me.

"Aha, just as I suspected OTC socks, all lawyers wear OTC socks Mr. Merrick," the inventor said gleefully and then my socks were off me.

I felt a cool draft around my feet as they were bared…

"So what of it?" I asked him, angry as hell now. "My wife bought me those socks man!! Shit, goddamned guy, you tricked me into this thing and then you take my shoes and socks off me??? What kind of pervert are you?"

(Like the monogrammed handkerchiefs I couldn't recall if my wife had given me the OTC Gold Toe socks as a birthday or anniversary gift. Like most wives she dutifully keeps her husband well-supplied in handkerchiefs, socks and underwear bud.) In response to my question I watched as Mr. Kujman sniffed the toes section of my dress socks, stretched them a bit from end to end, paired them, neatly folded them up and slipped them into his pants pocket, a look of pure ecstasy etched on his face.

"Stealing my damned socks, shit, of all things!" I grunted. "No wonder you brought me here in your hot car man! You wanted me cooked, good and sweaty and well-done so that my shoes and socks would stink like crazy!"

"Precisely, and if they smell this funky so early in the day I can only imagine how they must reek by the end of the day," the inventor quipped. "No wonder as you said, your wife complains when you remove your shoes at the end of the day…"

"Good laws man, that is so true," I said to the inventor. "She makes me put my socks directly into the washing machine. She won't even handle them. And you sniffed 'em like they were the best scented stuff in the world gads!!"

Then, he stepped back over to the egg shaped device and moved it forward till the tips of the feathers he had attached to it were grazing the bottoms of my feet.

""Oh gads," I whimpered.

"Did I happen to mention to you Mr. Merrick that the word "O-matic" is actually an abbreviation for what the machine is really called?" the inventor asked me, snickering.

"N-no, I don't think you did mention it," I responded sheepishly, stupidly wondering how I was going to explain my stolen socks to my wife when I got home, if I got home.

"Yes, that would be correct Mr. Merrick, because you see if I had told you what "O-matic" was an abbreviation for I highly doubt you would be sitting there now all strapped up and barefoot."

I simply stared blankly at the client who had become my captor…of all things.

"O-matic" is an abbreviation for what I call the "Laff-o-matic," Mr. Kujman explained.

"Th-the "Laff-o-matic?" I repeated, stammering out the word, my mind reeling at that point. "The Laff-o-matic???"

"Tell me Mr. Merrick, are you ticklish?" Mr. Kujman asked me and placed a fingertip against one of the buttons on the egg shaped device.

"Oh God Mr. Kujman, please, please not this," I said, almost crying now. "Yes, yes, I am so ticklish. I am so ticklish that it's awful. When my buddies in college found out how ticklish I was they made my life miserable because of it."

"Just as I hoped," the inventor said and pushed the button. "When I met you I somehow got the distinct feeling that you were a ticklish sort of fellow."

Suddenly, the feathers that he had attached to the hooks

at the end of the egg shaped device came to "fast" spinning life, rubbing hard against the bottoms of my bare feet as they revolved and revolved.

"Ohhhhhhhhhhhhhh God Ohhhhhhhhhhhh God no, not my feet, ha, ha, ha, ha, ha, ha, ha, ha, ha, ha, ha, ha, ha!!!!!" I suddenly guffawed in mad fits of laughter.

"Ah, I see that we're off to a superb demonstration Mr. Merrick," Mr. Kujman stated happily and tweaked one of my big toes.

"Y-you call this superb??? Oh God, ha, ha, ha, ha, ha, ha, ha, ha, ha, ha, ha, ha, ohhhhhhhhh God, t-turn it off, please Sir, turn it off!! Good laws, that thing is ticklin' my feet!!!" I railed. "Ha, ha, ha, ha, ha, ha, ha, ha, ha, ha, ha, ha, ha, ha!!!!!"

"And I will want to hear about your ticklish exploits with your college buddies later on Mr. Merrick," the inventor said, stepping next to me and tugging playfully at my necktie.

"L-later on? Ha, ha, ha, ha, ha, ha, ha, ha, ha, ha, ha, ha, ha, h-how long do you plan on keeping me here man???" I screeched.

"Well, in order to truly understand the "Laff-o-matic" and to have a thorough demonstration and to show you all the features of it I would have to say that the whole business day is called for Mr. Merrick," the inventor said and I thought for a second that I was hearing things.

"Th-the whole day???" I gasped. "The whole day??? HA, HA, HA, HA, HA, HA, HA, HA, HA, HA, HA, HA, HA, HA, ohhhhhhhhhhhh God, ha, ha, ha, ha, ha, ha, ha, ha, ha, ha, ha, ha!!!! Y-you actually plan to tickle my big ol' smelly feet all day??? G-gads, I'll laugh myself to death, ha, ha, ha, ha, ha, ha, ha, ha, ha, ha, ha, ha!!!!!!!"

"Well yes, and perhaps some overtime will be needed as well Mr. Merrick, this is a business deal after all, and you do need to understand the "Laff-o-matic" one hundred percent," Mr. Kujman said, running a hand over the top of my head and through my short hair.

"Some business deal, overtime too???" I guffawed madly, seething at the inventor at the same time. "Ha, ha, ha, ha, ha, ha, ha, ha, ha, ha, ha, ha, ha, ha!!!! I-I don't need to understand shit, ha, ha, ha, ha, ha, ha, ha, ha, ha, ha, ha!!!! I under-understand, gads, I understand that you tricked me into this blasted thing, ha, ha, ha, ha, ha, ha, ha, ha, ha, ha, ha, ha, ha, ha, ha!!!! I understand that you've kidnapped me in a way. I understand that you stole my socks!!! And more than anything I understand that I'm being tickle tortured here!!!! Ha, ha, ha, ha, ha, ha, ha, ha, ha, ha, ha, ha, ha, ha!!!!! Ohhhhhrrrrrrrrrrrr God damn it man!!! T-turn that wretched machine off man, and let me go!!!!"

As I yelled and laughed louder and louder I took awful note of the fact that the feathers attached to the hooks seemed to be spinning faster and faster. But Mr. Kujman hadn't touched any of the controls.

"It, it's spinning faster and faster," I gurgled, my hands balled into fists at my sides as I started sweating through my crisp white shirt. "Ha, ha, ha, ha, ha, ha, ha, ha, ha, ha, ha!!! H-how can that be??? Does this twisted gizmo have a mind of its own or something??? Oh good laws, ha, ha, ha, ha, ha, ha, ha, ha, ha, ha, ha, ha, ha, ha!!!!!"

"Now you see Mr. Merrick, that is exactly what I mean when I say that you need to understand the "Laff-o-matic" in full before you can issue me a patent for it," the inventor said to me, stepping back over to the egg shaped device and seeming to drink in the sight of me as I suffered in the throes of uncontrolled laughter.

Drinking in the sight of me, yes, that's what he was doing with a look of total contentment etched on his face. All the time since I had been introduced to him I had had the feeling that the inventor was somehow devouring me with his eyes. When he had met me he had no doubt chosen me as the victim for his newest creation's maiden voyage and I had stupidly allowed myself to be led on. Oh gads!!! Oh good laws!!! Why hadn't I paid attention to the warning signs and my lawyerly instincts??? Was I so desperate for the big fat commission that I would be getting for this assignment? Was all this worth it??? At that point in time however, with the way I was strapped and trapped there was no getting out of it anyway, the only way now was forward it seemed.

"Ha, ha, ha, ha, ha, ha, ha, ha, ha, ha, ha, ha, ha, ha, ha, ha, ha, ha!!!!!" I laughed louder and louder as the feathers spun faster and faster against the bottoms of my bare and smelly feet.

"The tickle mechanisms are equipped with sound sensors my dear attorney," the inventor said, suddenly looking real sinister and fiendish behind his thick glasses.

"S-sound sensors?" I gasped. "Ha, ha, ha, ha, ha, ha, ha, ha, ha, ha, ha, ha, ha, ha, ha, ha!!!! WH-what are the danged sound sensors for you twisted inventor??? Ha, ha, ha, ha, ha, ha, ha, ha, ha, ha, ha, ha, ha, ha, ha, ha, ha!!!!!"

"I must say, you certainly do ask the correct questions Mr. Merrick," Mr. Kujman chuckled and again tweaked one of my big toes, holding onto it a big longer this time. "The sound sensors are actually there so that the machine can hear the party participant as they squeal with laughter. As their laughter increases and gets louder as the participant is relentlessly tickled the machine speeds up."

As he spoke he twisted and yanked at my big toe that he was holding onto...

"H-holy tarnation and fucking shit!!!!" I crowed in a very Texas accent at that point (sounding embarrassingly like the cartoon character Yosemite Sam.) Ha, ha, ha, ha, ha, ha, ha, ha, ha, ha, ha, ha, ha, ha, ha, ha, ha, ha, ohhhhhhhhhhhh God!! D-do you mean to tell me here that the louder I laugh and chortle my damned head off the faster that thing is goin' to tickle my danged big smelly feet?"

"Precisely Mr. Merrick!!" the inventor said, tweaking my big toe even harder, seemingly proud of the fact that I had figured that much out. "I can see why you decided to become a lawyer!"

"Har, Har, Har, Har, Har, ha, ha, ha, ha, ha, ha, ha, ha, ha, ha, ha, ha!!!!!" I screamed like a hyena as the feathers spun faster and faster yet against my bare feet.

The inventor leaned down and stole a few sucks and suckles on my big toes, his eyes shut in ecstasy as he slurped at the cheesy jam of my smelly toes. It caused chills and thrills to course through me and made me laugh even louder... "P-perverted inventor, ha, ha, ha, ha, ha, ha, ha, ha, ha, ha, ha, ha, ha, s-s-suckin' at my danged toes," I grumbled heartily in laughter.

I knew that I had to calm my laughter down. There was no way that I could stop it completely, seeing as I'm highly ticklish. The inventor stopped sucking at my toes and watched as I laughed and laughed. He had chosen the right victim for this little party let me tell you. I would think that he had chosen me when Richards introduced me to him back at the office. I somehow wondered if Mr. Kujman had had his eye on Richards first, but then when he saw me twisted his plan around. Now I knew why the inventor had looked at me so hungrily. Gads!! I figured that if I calmed my laughter down a few notches at least that would slow the mechanism down... But that was easier said than done bud, seeing as the way I was presently being tickled was causing me to laugh harder and harder and louder and louder... Oh gads!!!

"Ha, ha, ha, ha, ha, ha, ha, ha, ha, ha, ha, ha, ha, ha, ha, ha, ha!!!!" I crowed and cawed loudly, but then with a hard and sheer effort I took a deep breath in between laughing, pursed my lips together and did my goddamned best to stifle my laughter.

"PPPPPPHHHHHFFFFFFF!!!" was the sound that escaped from between my lips at the point.

As I tried my best to stifle my laughter I thought just how comical it would have been had it been Richards who wound up in this predicament rather than me, his pee-on so to speak. I would bet that the fucking top partner in the firm would have insisted on Mr. Kujman tickle torturing him for all of two days, seeing as that was the kind of ass kisser he was, and not to mention that he had huge feet that could be tickled for that amount of time very easily.

"PPPPPHHHHHFFFFF!!!" I sputtered again, stifling my laughter some more.

Mr. Kujman looked at me suspiciously and quickly figured out what I was attempting to do.

"Hee, hee, hee, hee, hee, hee, hee," I laughed much softer then, causing the danged "Laff-o-matic" to slow down considerably. "Hee, hee, hee, hee, hee, hee, hee, hee…"

A look of victory came into my eyes…

But then, the inventor stepped to a small chest of drawers, opened the top drawer and took out a smooth stick, the type of smooth stick that a doctor uses to depress your tongue when lookin' down your throat during a medical examination. With a look of the utmost determination Mr. Kujman stepped next to my being tickled feet.

"Wh-what???" I gasped as he grabbed one of my big toes, yanked it aside and slid the stick back and forth against the tender flesh between my toes. "OOOOOOHHHHRRRRR NO NO!!!! HA, HA, HA, HA, HA, HA, HA, HA, HA, HA, HA!!!!!" He moved to my next toe and yanked that one aside and slid the smooth stick between that one and the next one next. I guffawed loud laughter, even louder than before…

"Ha, ha, ha, ha, ha, ha, ha, ha, ha, ha, ha, ha, ha, ha!!!!" I screamed as the "Laff-o-matic" sped up again and the feathers did their dirty work against the bottoms of my feet as Mr. Kujman tormented me between the toes with that smooth stick. "Ohhhhrrrrrrrr good laws man, th-that's a dirty trick to've played on me!! Ha, ha, ha, ha, ha, ha, ha, ha, ha, ha, ha, ha, ha, lemme outa here you blasted sicko!!"

As I laughed and laughed Mr. Kujman tickled between the toes of my right foot as the toes of my left foot twitched and flicked involuntarily with a life of their own it seemed…

"Har, har, har, har, har, ohhhhrrrrrrr har, har, har!!!!!" I crowed like crazy as the inventor held my pinky toe yanked away from the one before it and slid that danged stick between them relentlessly. "Ha, ha, ha, ha, ha, ha, ha, ha, ha, ha, ha, ha, ha!!!!! Th-that danged stick ain't a part of your device Mr. Kujman!! Using that thing on me to get me laughing louder is what I would call dirty pool!! Ha, ha, ha, ha, ha, ha, ha, ha, ha, ha, ha, ha!!!!"

"I must say, I've always believed that the sound of a young man in the throes of uncontrollable laughter is truly music to my ears," Mr. Kujman said and then started trailing his stick between the toes of my left foot.

"Gl-glad you think so Sir!! Ha, ha, ha, ha, ha, ha, ha, ha, ha, ha, ha, ha, ha!!!!" I replied. "Because right now that's just what the hell I am, ha, ha, ha, ha, ha, ha, ha, ha, ha, ha, ha, ha!!!!!"

The "Laff-o-matic spun the feathers faster and faster as I laughed louder and louder…

"What I am glad for Mr. Merrick is that this demonstration is going so well," the inventor chuckled.

"B-but, ha, ha, ha, ha, ha, ha, ha, ha, ha, th-there's no need to be ticklin' me with that stick Mr. Kujman," I repeated and pleaded. "It, it's not part of the machine… Ohhhhrrrr good laws!!!"

"No, that is true my dear attorney," the inventor said and continued ticklin' between my toes anyway. "But the object of the game with the "Laff-o-matic" is to keep the participant laughing as loudly as possible."

"Ha, ha, ha, ha, ha, ha, ha, ha, ha, ha, ha, ha, ha, ha, ha!!!!! Fuccccckkkk!! S-so glad you tell a guy the rules of a game after the fact," I laughed and screeched my words in my Texas accent.

He tickled between all my toes a total of three times on each foot, going back and forth and back and forth between my big ol' size ten and a half's. By then I was sopped in sweat and I came to the horrid realization that I was sporting a piss filled hard-on in my suit pants.

"Ha, ha, ha, ha, ha, ha, ha, ha, ha, ha, ha, ha, ha, ha, ha, ha, ha, ha!!!!" I laughed and laughed, watching as Mr. Kujman put the smooth stick back in the drawer and my eyes opened wide in horror when I saw him take out a thick bristled hairbrush. "Har, har, har, har, har, har, har, n-no!! You wouldn't!! Ohhhhrrrr g-gads, what a fucked up way to treat your attorney man!!"

Grinning from ear to ear he stepped over to the egg shaped device, pushed a button on it and the thing slid downwards, causing the feathers to tickle the lower portions of the bottoms of my big ol' feet, mostly my heels.

"Ha, ha, ha, ha, ha, ha, ha, ha, ha, ha, ha, ha, ha, ha, ha, ha, ha!!!!" I laughed loudly as the skin on my heels is coarse and very, very sensitive, like most people's I would guess.

Not to have the top portions of the bottoms of my feet feel left out Mr. Kujman began rubbing the thick bristles of the hairbrush lightly against them, back and forth and back and forth in a rhythmic motion.

"OOOOOOOOOOOOOO no, no!!!" I gurgled helplessly. "Ha, ha, ha, ha, ha, ha, ha, ha, ha, ha, ha, ha, ha, ha, ha, ha, ha!!!! Br-brushin' my danged feet... Ha, ha, ha, ha, ha, ha, ha, ha, ha, ha, ha, ha, ha, ha, ha!!!!"

As the feathers tickled my heels and Mr. Kujman

brushed, brushed, brushed the balls and upper portions of my feet all ten of my toes twitched and flicked like crazy now. My piss hard-on was more than evident in my suit pants at that point as well. Gads, I was totally tented up bud. Mr. Kujman would have some devious and sinister tickling plans for my huge Texas beef very soon too let me tell you… Oh my word!!! Tickling my feet was just the beginning of what would be a long and drawn out workday for me… What a way to make a living! Finally, oh finally, after about forty-five minutes to an hour of non-stop tickling Mr. Kujman put the hairbrush away and pushed the "stop" button on the egg shaped device. The feathers stopped tickling my feet… For those last forty-five minutes to the hour all I had done was laugh and laugh and laugh and laugh. As the inventor brushed my feet and the feathers did their dirty work I have to admit that there wasn't all that much to talk about bud…

"Ha, ha, ha, ha, ha, ha, ha, ha, ha, ha, ha, ha, hee, hee, hee, hee, hee…" I laughed softer and softer as the sensations coursing through me slowly subsided.

I sat there all strapped up, sweating and with a danged piss hard-on tenting my suit pants as the inventor opened a small refrigerator and took out two half-gallon size bottles of mineral water. I couldn't help noticing the tips of my Gold Toe socks sticking out of his pocket as he bent to get the water. Fucking guy, of all things, he steals my danged smelly socks…

"Thirsty Mr. Merrick?" the inventor asked me, stepping next to me as he took the cap off the first bottle.

"I would say so Mr. Kujman," I replied and he inserted an extra long straw into the first half-gallon bottle and held the thin strand to my lips.

I sipped the water down slowly, it was ice fucking cold,

but refreshing and maddening at the same time, seeing as it made me have to piss even more bud… Have you ever had to piss like crazy and then made the mistake of drinking some real cold water? Big mistake bud, real big fucking mistake let me tell you. The inventor held a hand against the back of my neck, kneading it with his thumb as he force-fed me the water. When I tried to slip the straw out from between my lips he held the bottle tighter and pressed forward with it so that the straw was inserted back into my mouth. His hand behind my neck was still icy cold and sent chills through me as he squeezed and caressed the back of my neck. I wasn't thrilling all that much to him caressing me and ruffling my hair as he had done, but in the position he had me in there wasn't all that much that I could do to stop him. The coldness of his hand on the back of my neck combined with the ice cold mineral water he was literally forcing me to drink caused me to have to piss even more.

"I truly am so glad that all this worked out Mr. Merrick," the inventor said and momentarily allowed me to slip the straw out from between my lips so that I could breathe.

"Yeah, I suppose you could say that," I replied and he quickly slid the straw back between my lips.

I shook my head "no" but Mr. Kujman said "Down the hatch Mr. Merrick" with total authority in his voice. With no choice in the matter I sipped down the ice cold mineral water through the straw, my insides churning when half the bottle was done. As I drank and drank my piss hard-on grew more agonizingly stiff and rigid.

"M-Mr. Kujman, please Sir," I panted when he again slid the straw into my mouth and force fed me the last of the half gallon of water.

I looked miserably over at the other bottle which he had

placed on a nearby shelf. If the need to piss was miserable earlier, it was agonizing now to the point of madness.

"So uh, so now that you've demonstrated your device I would like to get some pictures of it, start the paperwork, and use the bathroom," I said as he quickly dumped the empty water bottle in a trash bin and stepped back over to me. "So if you would be so kind to undo the straps I'll…"

"I'll get the pictures Mr. Merrick," the inventor said with that tone of authority again. "All you have to do is laugh…"

That said he pressed the start button on the egg shaped device and the feathers returned to spinning life.

"Ohhhhhhhhhhhhhrrrr gads, no, no, not again, ha, ha, ha, ha, ha, ha, ha, ha, ha, ha, ha, ha, ha!!!!! Ohhhhhrrrrrrrr God, th-this is awful man!!! Ha, ha, ha, ha, ha, ha, ha, ha, ha, ha, ha, ha, ha, ha!!!!" I chortled mightily in my Texas accent as I was suddenly being tickle tortured anew.

He pressed another button on the device and the thing slid back up so that the feathers were again tickling the upper portions of my feet. I laughed louder and louder and the feathers spun faster and faster. Obviously the sound sensors were working very adequately in there… I watched as the inventor snapped my attaché case open and found my digital camera.

"No, no, ha, ha, ha, ha, ha, ha, ha, ha, ha, ha, ha, ha, ha, ha!!!!" I laughed and crowed. "I-I only need pictures of the device, ha, ha, ha, ha, ha, ha, ha, ha, ha, ha, ha!!!!! I don't need any pictures of me sufferin' in it!! Ha, ha, ha, ha, ha, ha, ha, ha, ha, ha, ha, ha, ha!!!!"

"I need these pictures Mr. Merrick," the inventor said and as he aimed my camera at me I heard it clicking. I could barely see for the tears in my eyes as I laughed and laughed and laughed.

"OHHHHRRRRRRR ha, ha, ha, ha, ha, ha, ha, ha, ha, ha, ha, ha, ha, ha, ha, ha, ha, ha!!!!!" I laughed and laughed, facing forward as he snapped picture after picture of me.

"These shots will insure your silence over this whole experience and will also insure your return here when I need a participant to demonstrate the device for potential buyers," he said fiendishly.

"Wh-what???" I gasped and turned and looked at him total horror.

He snapped a good picture of my shocked and laughing expression…

Good God and almighty man, not only had the wacky inventor tricked and kidnapped my handsome ass, he also planned to blackmail me, oh fuck!! When he had enough pictures of me in the uncontrollable throes and fits of laughter he put my camera back in my attaché case and then stepped to my side. Even though he had returned the camera to my case I knew that he wouldn't allow for me to get my hands on it ever again. Good laws, after all this the first thing I would buy with my commission check would have to be a new camera.

"Okay Mr. Merrick, it's now time for the next phase of the demonstration of my "Laff-o-matic" device," the inventor said and brazenly began unbuttoning my sweat sopped crisp white dress shirt from under the binding straps, yanking my silk necktie aside as well.

"WH-what are you doing???" I gasped. "Ha, ha, ha, ha,

ha, ha, ha, ha, ha, ha, ha, ha, ha, ha, ha, ha, ha ohhhhhhrrrr gads, wh-what now man??? What now???"

When he saw the white cotton tee shirt under my dress shirt he looked dismayed for a second. He seemed to be mulling over his options and then gripped the top portion of my tee shirt at the neck. With a mighty pull he tore my tee shirt straight down the center, exposing my rock hard muscular chest and my big ol' man nips.

"Ohhhhhhhhhhhhrrrrr, ha, ha, ha, ha, ha, ha, ha, ha, ha, ha, ha, wh-what is this shit???" I guffawed angrily, looking down at my now unbuttoned pulled apart dress shirt, my askew necktie and my torn tee shirt. "S-strippin' me down like some cheap whore or somethin'?"

What a sight I truly was bud, totally unprofessional and out of uniform for a lawyer...

"Ah, just as I had hoped for Mr. Merrick," the inventor said happily, almost sadistically actually, just about breathlessly as he meanly handled my man nips with his thumbs and first two fingers, squeezing the hell out of them, twisting them, yanking at them. "Very nice, very big, very pointy and very meaty bulbous nipples...just as I hoped for."

"H-hey, get your hands off my man nips you pervert, this has gone far enough now!" I ranted as another bout of laughter captured me. "Ha, ha, ha, ha, ha, ha, ha, ha, ha, ha, ha, ha, ha, ha!!!!!!"

"Not nearly far enough my dear attorney," the inventor said, let go of my nipples and squatted down at the egg shaped device at my left side.

"Ohhhhhhhhhhhhhrrrrr g-gads, wh-what now???" I repeated miserably, the tingling sensations coursing through my man nips unnerving me from the inventor's touch. "Ha, ha, ha, ha, ha, ha, ha, ha, ha, ha, ha, ha, ha, ha, ha, ha, ha, ha, ha!!!!!!"

Granted, what he had said was true bud, good laws yes. My nipples are of the silver dollar and jumbo size, big and round and pink man, real pink and pointy, bulbous, to coin his word. When he was handling them it took his thumbs and more than one finger to really work them. My wife calls 'em fleshy while I refer to them as my man nips. I wouldn't ever call them my tits; that sounds too womanly bud. (One of my so called good buddies back in college called 'em my big ol' titty tits. Hell of a way to refer to a guy's nipples huh?) They adorn my slightly hairy and very muscular barrel-like chest, two big pink pencil erasers they look like. Now the insane inventor was planning to somehow tickle torture my hefty man nips, oh gads!! He raised the egg shaped device till it was adjacent to my left nipple, the hook-like claws on the end of it pointing directly at my poor nub. I didn't need three educated guesses of what I was in for next bud. As my feet were tickled more and more I watched as the inventor then stepped to the right side of me. Again he squatted down and got the other egg shaped device situated just like the one on my left side, the hook-like claws of the thing pointing directly at my right nipple in this case. As I laughed and laughed, I watched in horror as he opened another drawer in the chest of tickle supplies I nearly blanched.

"HAR, HAR, HAR, HAR, HAR, HAR, HAR, HAR, HAR, HAR, HAR," I laughed loudly and in terror when I saw that what he had taken from the drawer were two electronic manicure files with round buffered tops attached to them. "Ohhhhhhhrrrrrr God no, no Mr. Kujman, please!!" I pleaded crazily. "Ha, ha, ha, ha, ha, ha, ha, ha, ha, ha, ha, ha, ha, ha, ha, ha, ha, ha!!!!!"

He stepped first to the left sided egg shaped device that

was aimed at my nipple on that side. Sitting there strapped up tight I couldn't do anything except laugh as he attached the manicure file to the hook and pressed the round buffered top if it to my nipple.

"No, no, no, ohhhhhhhrrrr gads, ha, ha, ha, ha, ha, ha, ha, ha, ha, ha, ha, ha, ha!!!" I laughed, almost crying now.

He quickly stepped to the right side of the device and did the same thing with the other electronic manicure file. In between my hysterical bouts of laughter I gulped hard a couple of times. If my wife were able to she would tell you guys out there reading this just how very sensitive to the touch my big fat nipples are. While her and I are havin' sex she knows that just a slight squeeze or lick on my big ol' man nips is enough to get my Texas beef harder than a rock and pulsin' bud. I shouldn't be giving out my and my wife's bedroom secrets here, but in the position I'm in I don't think she'll be all that riled with me for doing so. While I'm making love to her she'll squeeze my big man nips to really get me pounding away inside her. And good laws, even after I've cum she'll do this thing that'll totally make me crazy bud. After I've shot my load inside her she'll squeeze my man nips real hard before I can slip my spent Texas beef out of her. Her squeezing my man nips gets me all worked up and hard all over again man. I cannot describe for you just how fucking intense and mind-blowing it is to be made hard all over again right after having shot my load. When I'm hard again from having my man nips squeezed the wife knows that I'm good for another round. Damn, but according to my wife my man nips are like two control knobs for my big ol' Texas beef bud. What the inventor was about to do to them was unthinkable though, but again, given the position I was in there wasn't much I could do about it man...

"Ha, ha, ha, ha, ha, ha, ha, ha, ha, ha, ha, ha, ha!!!!" I crowed crazily as the inventor held a fingertip over the button that controlled the hooks the manicure buffers were attached to.

"P-please don't, oh God no!!" I gurgled as he leered lecherously at me. "I have such ticklish and sensitive man nips, oh gads!!!"

But then, he pressed the button and to my surprise both of the manicure files came to spinning life, at high fucking speed bud, oh good laws!!! The buffered tops of the things spun crazily against the sides and tips of my poor man nips, rotating around and around and around my nubs...

"OHHHHHRRRRRRRRRR!!!!!!! Ha, ha, ha, ha, ha, ha, ha, ha, ha, ha, ha, ha, ha, ha!!!!!" I laughed insanely now, my voice and screams seeming to fill the workshop which had become my prison. "NO, NO, not my man nips and my feet at the same danged time man!!"

"Perfect demonstration I would say Mr. Merrick," the wacky inventor said to me, pulling my tie playfully.
"Gl-glad you think so man," I cackled crazily. "G-gads, it feels like you're roasting my man nips Mr. Kujman!! Ha, ha, ha, ha, ha, ha, ha, ha, ha, ha, ha, ha, ha, ha, ha!!!!"

Looking down I watched as the round buffered tops of the manicure files did their dirty work tickling my man nips. When they rotated around like two things alive against the sides of my nubs and then spinning like crazy against the tips of my man nips I thought for sure that I would go crazy with laughter. It was beyond maddening watching those things spin and spin all around and against my nips tips.

"The devices at your sides work on the same level as the one tickling your feet Mr. Merrick," the inventor stated.
"S-sound sensors?" I asked him, glancing at him and then back

down again as I was relentlessly tickled. "Ha, ha, ha, ha, ha, ha, ha, ha, ha, ha, ha, ha, ha, ha, ha!!!!"

"Precisely," Mr. Kujman said happily. "Now I can honestly say that you are getting a proper demonstration."

"L-lucky me huh?" I asked him sarcastically. "Ha, ha, ha, ha, ha, ha, ha, ha, ha, ha, ha, ha, ha, ha!!!!!"

As the manicure files buffered tops worked my nipples I felt the tingling sensations all the way down to my piss hard cock in my suit pants. Gads, that's the effect that having my man nips worked over has on me bud, it always more than plumps up my Texas beef, no matter what. It made me tent up even more, and not to mention the fact that by then the half gallon of mineral water had cascaded through me and I had to piss worse than a racehorse at that point. I figured that if I told the inventor of my need to relieve myself that he would have to set me free, and then at least this awful experience would be over. I mean, did he really, really plan on tickle torturing me all day?" I mean, come on, let's be reasonable about this... Tickle torturin' some poor attorney all day is just unthinkable, ain't it? "M-Mr. Kujman," I sputtered in between laughing and laughing. "Ha, ha, ha, ha, ha, ha, ha, ha, ha, ha, ha, ha, ha, ha, ha, ha, ha!!!!!"

"Yes Mr. Merrick?" he asked me in reply, seeming to be reading my mind and looking somewhat hungrily at the big tent in my suit pants.

"I-I need to take a leak man!!!! Ha, ha, ha, ha, ha, ha, ha, ha, ha, ha, ha, ha, ha, ha, ha, ha!!!! We're talking a big time leak at that too..." I cried out hysterically. "After all that water you made me drank I doubt I'll be able to hold it much longer Sir!! Ha, ha, ha, ha, ha, ha, ha, ha, ha, ha, ha, ha, ha, ha, ha!!!!"

"Ah, also something that I wanted to hear my dear attorney," the inventor said happily, clapping his hands together. "There's time enough for that though. For now you'll have to hold your water so to speak."

"Ha, ha, ha, ha, ha, ha, ha, ha, ha, ha, ha, ha, ha, ha, ha, ha!!!! Wh-what???" I gasped in utter disbelief at what he had just said. "Ohhhhhrrrrrrrr gads, what a fucked up day this turned out to be for me man!!"

Once again Mr. Kujman got the smooth tongue depressing stick and meanly tickled between my toes with the damned thing. Each time he squeezed one of my toes to yank it aside I squealed in louder and louder fits of laughter. It seemed that I was becoming more and more sensitive to any touch at that point. And the inventor handling my toes proved that point bud. The sound sensors on the "Laff-o-matic" heard me very well and all the attachments on the device spun faster and faster, tickling the tar out of my feet and man nips. Watching those buffered manicure files rotating around and around my man nips was maddening bud…totally fucked up… Every time they settled on the very tips of my poor man nips and rotated faster and faster and faster against them I laughed louder and louder. It was a combination of having my man nips tickle tortured and out-rightly roasted and toasted feeling and the way that Mr. Kujman was again ticklin' between my toes with that tongue depressor that had me laughing and feeling even more sensitive to the touch at that point. I think that I was definitely finding out that if you relentlessly tickle tortured a guy for long periods of time he did indeed become more and more sensitive to the touch. What a fucked up education I was getting in the laws of tickling tortures. Good fucking laws!!!
"HA, HA, HA, HA, HA, HA, HA, HA, HA, HA, HA, HA, HA, HA, HA, HA!!!!! I-I gotta pee man!!!" I screamed, all sweaty and stinky now, sounding like Forrest Gump as I told the inventor

that "I had to pee."

"All in good time Mr. Merrick," Mr. Kujman said and slid the tongue depressor through the sections between my toes relentlessly. "All in good time..."

After another forty-five minutes to an hour or so of relentless tickle torture the inventor again turned off the "Laff-o-matic" device. The feathers stopped tickling my feet and the round buffers on the manicure files stopped tickling my man nips.

"Ohhhhhhhhhhh, oh man, oh gads, good laws, hee, hee, hee, hee, hee, hee, hee, hee, hee," I laughed softly again as the sensations still coursed through me, even though I wasn't being tickle tortured at that moment...nope, not at the moment bud, but soon, very soon I would be again...

Mr. Kujman didn't believe in wasting time nor did he believe in not tickling me... My nipples had been unbelievably jutted up to twice their size from those danged buffered things rotating so relentlessly against them all that time. No amount of fondling and squeezing of them that my wife ever did got them so swollen and jutted bud. Gads, at that moment I must have had two of the most sensitive and sexy feelin' man nips on the planet...

I watched as Mr. Kujman picked up the second half gallon bottle of mineral water, opened it, and slipped a long straw into it. He approached me with the bottle of water.

"M-Mr. Kujman Sir, I-I really don't think it's a good idea to water me again," I drawled miserably in my Texas accent, the need to piss beyond maddening at that point. "Th-the way I need to take a leak drinking that cold water will make it worse Sir."

Without a word he grabbed the back of my neck real tight, forced my head slightly back and held the straw in the bottle to my trembling lips.

"S-sir?" I gurgled and then found myself sipping down the second bottle of mineral water.

"Making you have to piss even more is part of the game-plan my dear attorney," the inventor said and forced me to sip down just about the entire second bottle of mineral water. By then my cock felt all bloated and beyond piss filled in my suit pants…

My head was spinning and I had the feeling that I could float away I had drank so much mineral water…

I had to wonder how making a guy wait to piss would be a fun part of a party where he was tickle tortured in the "Laff-o-matic."

When I was done drinking the water the inventor disposed of the second bottle and then to my horror I watched as he stepped next to me and started pulling the fly zipper down on my suit pants.

"H-hey, HEY!!! Wh-what do you think you're doin' now you madman???" I screamed irately.

He reached into the fly opening of my suit pants (not all that gently I might add) and past my frosty white boxer shorts and brought out my over-sized pride and joy, what I call my Texas beef (as you know) along with my two big succulent the size of kiwis furry balls.

"Ohhhhhhhhhhrrrr fuck man, handlin' my damned beefy

Texas tube steak!!" I raged breathlessly as the inventor held my cock tightly in his hand, hefting my balls outside my suit pants. My nine inch cut Texas beef was harder than a rock, piss fucking hard to be exact, thick veins pulsed at its shaft all around it, beads of piss (and pre cum man, oh gads pre cum too) oozed from my wide sexy slit. My cock and balls were as sweaty as the rest of me at that point and the man scent emanating from them was musty and sexy all at the same time, something else about me that the wife adores bud... With a deep breath and a gasp emanating from him Mr. Kujman gave my pride and joy a fast squeeze, getting a good loud gasp out of me too bud...

"Ohhhhhhh gads man, leggo of my Texas beef," I garbled. "Pervert that you are!!"

"Okay Mr. Merrick, a few more moments and then I'll allow you to relieve yourself," the inventor said, let go of my cock and stepped over to a cabinet of supplies.

The feathers were still pressed against my bare feet and the round buffers were still pressed against the sides of my nipples, teasing me, letting me know that more tickle torture was yet to come...

"Alright then Mr. Merrick, we will begin with this," Mr. Kujman said and took something out of the supply cabinet and quickly stepped behind me before I could see what it was.

Before I could utter a word he strapped a ball-gag with a small breathing hole in its center into my mouth.

"Hmmmmmmfff???" I asked stupidly as he secured the thing around the back of my neck.

"This won't last long Mr. Merrick, just until you've relieved yourself," the inventor said, sounding totally sadistic as he stepped back over to the supply cabinet.

"HRRRRRFFFFFF!!!" I garbled against the ball-gag, watching intently this time at what he took from the supply cabinet next.

When I saw the next item he took out my heart thundered in my chest... Holding it up for me to see the inventor said, "Mr. Merrick, this is a Ferguson catheter." As he stepped back over to me again I took in the fact that the "Ferguson Catheter" was actually a long rubber see-through tube with a latex sheath at the end of it. My eyes were opened wide in total terror at the possibilities of the thing. He wouldn't I was thinking, he just wouldn't... I squirmed miserably under the binding straps as he did. He expertly slid the latex sheath over my cock head, fitting it snugly on it. It felt like a condom on there actually but a lot tighter... The thing hugging my hard, hard cock made me even more breathless...

"HHHRRRRFFFF..." I gurgled miserably as he then inserted the end of the see-through tube into the breathing hole of the ball-gag.

FUCK!! He was plannin' on making me drink my piss! What a fucked up way for a guy to relieve himself I thought crazily. I looked at the inventor with rage in my eyes.

"Okay then Mr. Merrick, now you know why I force fed you so much mineral water," he said to me and grabbed the end of the tube just a few scant inches away from my latex sheath covered cock head. "This is called "water reclamation" in case you didn't know it. After you've consumed your urine we'll repeat this procedure one more time after you've been thoroughly tickle tortured again and then the third time you'll relieve yourself in a more traditional fashion."

As he spoke he was stroking the tube close to my cock, the sensations causing me to piss...

"HHHRRRRRFFFF..." was all I could say as my piss slowly began trickling through the tube and upwards toward my ball-gagged mouth.

"Too many times of water reclamation can after a while cause serious poisoning," the inventor said as I watched my rancid frothy piss trickling closer to my mouth. "And we wouldn't want that now would we Mr. Merrick? After all, this is simply a demonstration and all in fun here after all..."

And what a fucked up demonstration it had turned out to be bud. I wanted to rant at him all kinds of obscenities, all kinds of curse and swear words, but then, oh gads, then, I was getting the first tastes and throat fills of my warm frothy piss.

"GGGRRRRRRRRHHHH!!!!" I garbled miserably as I had no choice in the matter but to slake down my own piss. "Good, the Ferguson Catheter is working perfectly," the inventor said happily.

I watched as my piss seemed to be speeding through the tube at that point as I pissed uncontrollably it seemed. The inventor squeezed my sweaty balls a few times which seemed to coax me along all the more. I didn't lose a drop of my piss that was for sure. It tasted rancid and sour...

GLUB GLUB GLUB was the embarrassing sounds that came from my throat each time I swallowed another mouthful of my frothy piss...

When I was done pissing it felt like it was hours later. Gads, it had to be the longest piss I had ever taken and I had been the damned urinal of all things. The inventor first took the latex sheath off my cock head. It looked all bloated and sort of puffed up I suppose from the tightness of the sheath having been so snug on it. He then took the end of the see through tube out of the ball-gag and put the "Ferguson Catheter" down on a nearby table. When he took the ball-gag out of my mouth I licked my lips before ranting at him.

"Y-you sick and mad inventor!!!" I railed at him. "Y-you made me drink my own piss you madman!!"

"Yes Mr. Merrick, and if you would please take note your "Texas beef" as you call it is still hard and pulsing," the inventor stated, looking hungrily at my pride and joy. "Now for the next phase of helping you to relieve yourself we are going to play a guessing game here."

"A guessing game? Helping me to relieve myself?" I asked him miserably. "You call this helping me? Helping me would be letting me out of here man!! Oh good laws, what next??"

As I spoke and ranted I couldn't help but notice that my mouth tasted all sour and vile from having scoffed down my own damned piss…

In a fast move the inventor took my long white handkerchief out of the pocket of my suit jacket hanging on the back of the chair that I was so expertly strapped into. In an even faster move he tied the handkerchief over my eyes, blindfolding me just as he had done earlier when he'd brought me in there.

"A-a guessing game now huh?" I asked as I was plunged into darkness.

"Yes, within a few moments you are going to hear a sound," the inventor explained to me. "It will be your job to identify what that sound is."

"And then you'll let me go?" I asked him hopefully.

"No, then I'll let you relieve yourself some more, but not of the need to piss this time," the inventor chuckled and I again heard the sound of a drawer opening and then closing. "Are you ready to play the guessing game Mr. Merrick?"

"I-I guess I don't have all that much choice now do I Mr. Kujman?" I asked him in reply, feeling totally mortified, totally on display and totally terrorized at this point.

"Alright then Mr. Merrick, please if you would, identify this sound," the inventor said and I heard a button clicked.

What I heard next was the sound of a loud buzzing, a rotating kind of buzzing actually…

I thought about it for a second or two and then stupidly blurted out, "That's an electric toothbrush Mr. Kujman! OOOOOOOO no…"

"Very well done Mr. Merrick," the inventor said gleefully and whipped the blindfold off me, leaving it dangling around my neck that time.

I looked at him and sure enough he was holding up a soft bristled electric toothbrush. It was switched on to high speed and the bristles on the danged thing were vibrating madly, teasing me already.

"WH-what are you plannin' on doin' with that man???" I asked him miserably; not even wanting to contemplate the possibilities. "It's bad enough you made me drink my own danged piss!! What now???"

"Heh, as if you need for me to tell you Mr. Merrick," the inventor said and pressed the button to start the devices tickling my nipples again.

"Ha, ha, ha, ha, ha, ha, ha, ha, ha, ha, ha, ha, ha, ha, ha, ha, ha, ha, ha, ha, ha, ha ohhhhhhhrrrrrr no, no, not again you madman!!" I screeched.

Mr. Kujman quickly stepped to the foot of the device and flicked on the machine that controlled the feathers.

"HAR, HAR, HAR, HAR, HAR, HAR, HAR, HAR, HAR, HAR!!!!!" I squealed like crazy all over again, my feet and man nips being relentlessly tickled.

But this time as I was tickled I watched as my hard Texas beef did a sexy and stupid dance between my legs, my balls churning and resting outside my suit pants.

"Okay then Mr. Merrick, it's time to rid you completely for the moment of that pesky feeling of having to relieve yourself," the inventor said and moved to my crotch, holding the toothbrush up, and then moving it slowly and menacingly toward my big pride and joy.

"OHHHHHHHHHH no, no, th-that would be more than insane man!!" I guffawed. "Ha, ha, ha, ha, ha, ha, ha, ha, ha, ha, ha, ha, ha, ha, ha, ha, ha!!!!! Ohhhhhhhrrrrr fuck, what a shitty ass thing to do to me…"

Ignoring my pleas again the inventor pressed the soft vibrating bristles against the side of my big Texas beef and swirled them around and around and around it…

"RRRRRRRRRRRRRRRR geeeeeeeeez RRRRRRRRRR

RRRRR!!!!!" I screeched insanely through clenched teeth, looking up at the ceiling, my big hands balled into tight fists. "HA, HA, HA, HA, HA, HA, HA, HA, HA, HA, HA, HA, HA, HA, HA, HA, HA!!!! Ohhhhhrrrrrrr you fucker!! Y-you're ticklin' my damned cock, of all things, ohhhhrrrrrrr good laws man!!!!!"

I writhed and bucked miserably under the tight straps, trying to prevent myself from having the inevitable happen, namely that this would cause me to shoot my hefty load. But oh gads, the way that inventor was torturin' my cock there would be no holding it back let me tell you. I was a mess of goose bumps at that point and the need to shoot my load was overwhelming at that point. My cock felt beyond sensitive and sexy after having had that latex sheath over it and now that it was being worked with the toothbrush that made it all the more sensitive. Mr. Kujman saw how I was trying to hold it back so he meanly pressed the vibrating bristles harder against my shaft, moving the toothbrush slowly upwards, toward what I call my wide sexy slit. He erotically trailed the toothbrush bristles along the thick pronounced veins in my Texas beef, pressing it harder and harder against my poor shaft. Huge droplets of pre cum formed at the tip of my cock…

"Ha, ha, ha, ha, ha, ha, ha, ha, ha, ha, ha, ha, ha, ha, ha, ha, ha, ha, ha, ha!!!!!" I laughed and laughed like mad. "No, ohhhhrrrrrrr good laws no!!!"

Then, when I felt it and I knew that there was no holding it back I looked down at my poor suffering cock. The inventor rubbed the bristles two times against my wide sexy slit and that was all it took bud… I shot my thick creamy load like crazy…

"Ohhhhhhhhhhhrrrrrrrr fuck, fucker, fucker, fucker!!!!" I ranted crazily as he rubbed the vibrating soft bristles again against my shaft as I shot my pent-up load, bucking my head up and down, sweat dripping off me like crazy. "Goddamned pervert, slob!! Ha, ha, ha, ha, ha, ha, ha, ha, ha, ha, ha, ha, ha, ha, ha, ha, ha, ha, ha, ha!!!! J-just for the record Mr. Kujman, I ain't no danged homo!! You're working over the wrong damned guy here!!"

Then, all I could do was gasp and grunt, sounding like a real Texas cowboy as globs and globs of my sexy mess were extracted from me. I shot my thick creaminess all over the straps around my chest and even onto my suit pants... Good laws, how the fuck would I ever explain cum stains on my pants to the wife???

"ARRRRRRRHHHHH sh-shit, worse than when my college buds used to work me over man!!" I made the mistake of saying as still more of my good stuff erupted from my wide sexy slit.

When I was done shooting my load, I was totally breathless, and as I was still laughing like a hyena the wacky inventor went on and on rubbing the vibrating toothbrush bristles against the shaft of my now semi hardness.

"AYYYYYYRRRRR, gads, please stop Mr. Kujman, ohh-hhrrrrrr please stop!!!" I seethed; the sensations in my cock and being tickled nipples totally heightened after I shoot a load. "G-gads, I'm all sensitive and real sexy feelin' after I cum man... Ohhhrrrrrrr fuck, fuck, fuck man!!!"

As I swore like a captured soldier boy and struggled to no avail in the clutches of the "Laff-o-matic" the inventor took a moment to reach up and give one of my man nips a fast squeeze, and that was all it took bud...

"OHHHHHHHHHHHHHHH!!!!!" I bellowed at the surprise and shock of it all as the inventor knew my G-spot it seemed, that my man nips were the control knobs for my cock, as my wife had so aptly said.

He rubbed the soft vibrating bristles over my newly hard cock and grunting breathlessly and laughing at the same time I shot a second load...

"Ahhhhhhhhhhhhrrrrr fuck, talk about mortifying!" I gurgled as the second mess of my cum spurted all thick and creamy from my slit as the vibrating bristles did their relentless dirty work. "Ha, ha, ha, ha, ha, ha, ha, ha, ha, ha, ha, ha, ha, ha, ha, ha, ha, ha, ha, ha!!!!"

I came and came again all over my suit pants...

When I was done the scents of sweat, cum and the taste of piss in my mouth all mixed together was intoxicatingly sexy somehow...

Mr. Kujman again shut down the egg shaped devices and they stopped tickling me...

"Th-thank you, thank you man," I said softly, whimpering practically, my head hanging down.

When I looked up I saw that Mr. Kujman again had my camera in hand. I hadn't even heard him open my danged attaché case, good laws bud!!! I seethed angrily as he snapped a few pictures of me with my cock and balls totally on display, my suit pants drenched in sweat and cum... Now we were talking definite blackmail here...

When he was satisfied with the shots he had just gotten he put my camera back in my attaché case and looked me over appraisingly.

"Well, I must say that you're doing well so far Mr.

Merrick," he said, glancing at his watch. "And it's not that late in the afternoon just yet. We still have the rest of the day ahead of us. Isn't that wonderful?"

"Mr. Kujman, you can't mean that Sir," I pleaded, not looking at him, simply looking downwards. "I-I have to get back to the office, no, fuck that, I have to get home and clean myself up and get into a clean suit before my wife gets there to see me this way. And besides all that, I'm expected back at the office at some point today..."

"Yes, I will have to remedy that," he said softly. "I'll give you a ten minute break to catch your breath and compose yourself my dear attorney. While you do that I'll go upstairs and call Mr. Richards to let him know that our business here will take the better part of the day."

"WH-what???" I gasped loudly then, the sound of his words the worst of horrors at that moment. "Now see here, this has gone far enough..."

As I spoke he walked toward the door to the workshop.

"Oh, and you may yell all you would like to Mr. Merrick, just for your records where my device is concerned, this room is soundproof," the inventor said and closed the door behind him.

"DAMN!!!" I grunted angrily.

The inventor walked through the basement and up the stairs...

In the living room of his immense house Mr. Kujman sat on a small sofa and picked up the phone on the end table next to it. He dialed Mr. Gordon Richards directly, not even going through his secretary; he was the client after all. He had kid-napped me but he was the client. He had stolen my socks but he was the client. And damn, he had tickle tortured and terror-ized me, but he was the fucking client!!!!

"Hello? This is Gordon Richards," Gordon Richards answered on the first ring when he saw the inventor's phone number pop up on his caller ID box.

"Ah, Mr. Richards, how are you?" the inventor said jovially. "This is Lewis Kujman."

"Mr. Kujman, I'm doing great Sir, how are things pro-gressing at your end?" the top partner in the firm said just as jovially. "How is my man Byron Merrick doing with your license?"
"Fine, fine, I think that very soon we'll be able to start the paperwork," the inventor said happily. "It's just that the inspec-tion and the demonstration are taking a bit longer than we expected."

"Demonstration?" Gordon Richards asked.

"Well yes, you see your Mr. Merrick explained that he would need to see how the device I invented works," Mr. Kujman stated, sounding totally professional and businesslike.

"Okay, that's understandable," Mr. Richards replied.

"Well, when I explained to him that I hadn't planned on a demonstration and that I would have to contact an associate to serve as a volunteer for that purpose he graciously and most generously I might add volunteered to be the participant," Mr. Kujman went on.

"I see," Gordon Richards said, sounding unsure.

"So I just wanted to call and tell you how glad I am that your firm assigned this project to Mr. Byron Merrick, he's beyond professional in this regard," the inventor said with the utmost sincerity.

Mr. Richards's eyes lit up in delight…

"Well, that is what we aim for at the firm," he said, kissing the inventor's ass over the phone.

"So then it won't be a problem for you if I hold onto the young man for a while more Mr. Richards?" Mr. Kujman asked hopefully. "He really is doing so well with the entire project that I would hate to rush him through it and risk making a mistake perhaps. I do want everything to be on the up and up you understand."

"No, no, that's fine Sir, you can hold onto Merrick all day if needed," the top partner in the firm said, not knowing that he was signing my torture warrant so to speak. "He doesn't know it yet, but if he secures this deal with you to our satisfaction and yours he's going to be made partner."

"Well, that's wonderful to hear I must say," Mr. Kujman said grinning from ear to ear. "I'm so glad that I can be instrumental in furthering the young man's career."

"But please don't tell him that Sir," Gordon Richards said. "We want it to be a surprise around here when we tell him. I'm sure he'll be totally tickled over that."

"Yes, he will be tickled that I can assure you Mr. Richards," the inventor said, almost cracking up in laughter himself.

Gordon Richards didn't get the joke or it simply went over his ass kissing head...

"Very well then Mr. Richards, I'd best get back to the task at hand here," the inventor said. "And thank you again." "Thank you for calling Mr. Kujman, I'll have all of Byron's calls put on his voice mail for the remainder of the day."

The inventor hung up, grinned more-so from ear to ear and stood up...

He walked happily back toward the basement and the workshop...

As he came down the stairs he took my socks out of his pocket, sniffed them a few times and then quickly put them back into his pocket as he came back into the workshop...

"Ah, and here we are again Mr. Merrick," the inventor said happily. "Ten minutes exactly. I do hope you enjoyed your break."

"Yeah sure, it was time well spent," I said sarcastically in my thick Texas accent. "I was able to mull over some really important business situations that I have back at the office." "Well, all that will wait till tomorrow my dear attorney," Mr. Kujman said. "I just had a very nice chat with the top partner in your firm and he said that I could hold onto you all day, quote unquote..."

I looked at the inventor in total dismay as he stepped to the egg shaped device at my feet...

"Ready Mr. Merrick?" he asked me and pressed the "start" button.

"Ohhhhhhhhhhhhrrrrr no, no, and here we go again, dang it all!!!" I gurgled miserably, my toes coming to twitching life almost instantly as the feathers started spinning against the bottoms of my feet. "Ha, ha, ha, ha, ha, ha, ha, ha, ha, ha, ha, ha, ha, ha, ha, ha, ha, ha, ha, ha, ha ohhhhhhrrrrrrrrrr God!!" Quickly, he stepped to the egg shaped device that controlled the manicure file buffers and pressed the "start" button on that as well. Both egg shaped devices at my nipples came to spinning life again and then my poor man nips were again being tickled...

"AYYYYYYRRRRRRRR!!!!! Ha, ha, ha, ha, ha, ha, ha, ha, ha, ha, ha, ha, ha, ha, ha, ha!!!! I screamed. "D-did you tell Richards what the fuck you're doin' to me here???"

"Not totally," Mr. Kujman replied with a snide looking grin on his face. "Do you intend to tell him what I'm doing to you here today?"

In response I simply looked at him in total anger... He knew fully well that he would get away with all that he was doing to me there that day. He knew that I would never tell or report about the absurd situation I had so foolishly fallen into. And with the pictures he had taken of me he knew that my silence in the matter was totally insured...

"Do you intend to tell the top partner in your firm how you naively volunteered for a demonstration of my machine and wound up in the predicament you're now in?" he asked me meanly, almost laughing himself at that moment.

"RRRRRRRRR!!!!" I seethed miserably.

As I was being tickle tortured all over again I watched as the inventor attached more long sticks to the egg shaped devices that were being used to control the sticks tickle torturing my man nips. To these new sticks he attached two more manicure file buffers and to my horror he pressed them against my sensitive balls, holding my semi hardness by the very tip as he got them properly situated...

"Wh-what the fuck?" I ranted. "Ohhhhhhrrrrrrrrr, no, not my balls too you mad scientist inventor!" I sputtered helplessly as he teased my cock tip by giving it a squeeze or two. "Ha, ha, ha, ha, ha, ha, ha, ha, ha, ha, ha, ha, ha, ha, ha!!!!"

He pressed another button on one of the egg shaped devices and then the new attachments came to spinning life and my big sweaty balls were then being tickle tortured along with my feet and nipples...

"OHHHHHRRRRRRRR!!!! Ha, ha, ha, ha, ha, ha, ha, ha, ha, ha, ha, ha, ha, ha!!!!" I laughed louder and louder, just what Mr. Kujman wanted bud.

It caused the sound sensors to hear me and made the spinning devices rotate faster and faster with each passing second...

"AYYYYYYRRRRRRRR!!!!" I screamed as it felt like my balls were being vibrated to tickle torture death. "Ha, ha, ha, ha, ha, ha, ha, ha, ha, ha, ha, ha, ha, ha, ohhhhrrrr good laws, this is sick, sick, sick!!! Y-you're cookin' my danged balls with those things man!! Ha, ha, ha, ha, ha, ha, ha, ha, ha, ha, ha, ha, ha, ha, ha, ha, ha!!!!!"

Smiling from ear to ear the inventor stepped next to my upper strapped up torso...

"It's a demonstration Mr. Merrick," he said jovially and ruffled my sweat sopped short hair. "A demonstration that you asked for you might recall."

"I did at that didn't I?" I cackled miserably. "Ha, ha, ha, ha, ha, ha, ha, ha, ha, ha, ha, ha, ha, ha, ha, ha, ha!!!!! Ohhhhhhhrrrrrr gads, my poor feet, my poor man nips, my poor danged balls!!! Ha, ha, ha, ha, ha, ha, ha, ha, ha, ha, ha, ha, ha, ha, ha, ha, ha!!!!"

The sensations of the spinning buffers against my balls had them feeling like they were churning out of control in my sexy and sweaty sac... The same sensations caused my Texas beef to plump up good and hard and all juicy again...

"OHHHHHRRRRRRRR!!!! Ha, ha, ha, ha, ha, ha, ha, ha, ha, ha, ha, ha, ha, ha, ha, ha, ha, ha, ha, ha, ha!!!!" I laughed and laughed and laughed and laughed.

About an hour later Mr. Kujman decided to have some mercy on me, I supposed, as he turned off the egg shaped devices. The feathers at my feet and the manicure file buffers at my nipples and balls slowly came to a halt.
"Ohhhhhhhhh, th-thank you man, thank you, thank you," I blubbered, not really making any sense at all as I spoke at that moment, still twittering softly in laughter. "Hee, hee, hee, hee, hee, hee, hee, hee, hee, hee..."

When all the devices had stopped spinning I was a soaked in sweat mess, my crisp white shirt stuck to me, my suit pants stunk of sweat and cum and my feet were beyond ripe with the scent of my odor as well. My torn up tee shirt made me look like I had been worked over big time, actually in a way I was being worked over big time! Gads, it smelled worse than a locker room after a major league baseball or football game bud...and it was all me, unbelievably.

"Feeling alright?" the inventor asked me.

"Y-yeah, I-I suppose so," I replied, catching my breath.

"I'll get you some cold water and then we'll move on to the next phase of the demonstration Mr. Merrick," the inventor said, moving the feathers away from my bare feet.

"N-next phase?" I grunted miserably. "Man, I get the idea here!! This invention of yours is some piece of twisted shit!! Let me out of here, now!!!"

But instead he simply stepped over to the refrigerator and got a fresh half-gallon sized bottle of mineral water for me... My Texas tube steak twitched like crazy, the need to piss setting in again bud... Gads, just the thought of drinking my own piss down a second time sent awful chills through me... I sat docile and still as he again grabbed the back of my neck, tilted my head back and forced me to sip down the ice cold mineral water through a straw...

"Tastes good?" the inventor asked me, stroking the back of my head as I drank the water. I simply nodded and he forced me to scoff down the whole bottle...again... When I was done he put the empty bottle aside. I felt horribly bloated and over-stuffed. The gassy feeling coursing through me was like nothing I had ever felt before...

"Now, in order to earn a good half-hour or possibly more non tickle time I want to hear about how your college buddies worked you over in ticklish fashion," the inventor said, stepping up beside the "Laff-o-matic." "And I'll want to hear every minute detail. If you refuse to tell me what I want to hear I'll simply turn the device back on right now. It's your choice Mr. Merrick..." I gulped hard, belched loudly from all the water and piss flowing through me and looked up at my client, my client, the man who had become my captor...

"I'll tell you man, no problem at all," I said miserably and leaned my head back against the chair-back that I was strapped to. "Anything, anything to keep from being tickle tortured for any length of time man..."

"Ah, good, good Mr. Merrick," Mr. Kujman said to me, reached over and pulled on the lever next to the machine and that was attached to the upper portion of the chair that I was strapped to. "I see that you realize just how ticklish your situation is at this point. No pun intended."

After he pulled back on that lever the chair I was in started being moved backwards, stretching out my upper torso now along with my legs.

"H-hey, wh-what're you doin' man?" I blurted, sounding more annoyed than anything as I was laid out like a danged Thanksgiving turkey.

The device made a buzzing sound as I was stretched out good and tight into a taut prone position...

"Just making you a tad more comfortable Mr. Merrick," the inventor said, looking hungrily at my Texas beef as it stuck straight up, pointing all hard, erect and oozing pre cum and piss at the heavens.

"Ohhhhhrrrr gads, what next man?" I whimpered.

"Next you will tell me about your ticklish college exploits Mr. Merrick," the inventor said, tweaked one of my jutted up nipples and then let go of the lever that controlled the motion of my chair.

The chair stopped moving and the buzzing sound ended as well...

"I told you I would tell you man," I blubbered.

Dang it all man, I was really in a very vulnerable and sexy position now. All stretched out and strapped down, gads!! The inventor pulled up a chair next to the "Laff-o-matic" and I began one of the tickle stories of my past...nearly a tad more than ten years ago at that point... And I say "one of" the tickle stories of my past because there are a lot more than just this one bud. You see, after my so called buddy Mike and his brood found out just how ticklish I was they went out of their way numerous times to have some tickle torture fun with me. I'll relate those stories in the future if the need for them presents itself, and from all points with what Mr. Kujman has in mind for me I get the feeling that the need will be presenting itself to tell those tickle stories.

"I was nineteen years old at the time, a few weeks shy of my twentieth birthday to be exact," I began. "It was my second year in college... I had also decided to pledge a fraternity that year as well."

"What were you studying Mr. Merrick?" Mr. Kujman asked me.

"Business law," I replied, glancing at him as if he had just asked me the stupidest question in the world. "And I was also on the college's baseball team."

"You attended college in Texas Mr. Merrick?" Mr. Kujman asked me.

"Yes, I got my associate's and bachelor's degrees in Texas and my masters here in New York," I replied, looking at the man with my head turned toward him as I lay there totally helpless.

"What position did you play on the college's baseball team?" the inventor asked me.

"Batter," I replied. "Being on the baseball team was actually the reason I wound up being tickle tortured, me and my danged hero of the game homeruns man…"

"Ah, this should prove to be most interesting then," Mr. Kujman said, sounding elated. "A baseball hero being tickle tortured…"

"Yeah, great, just great, well like I said I was nearly twenty years old at the time," I went on miserably, but having no choice in the matter really. "My college was down to the season's last three games. We needed to win two more of them against two different teams in order to be the state's college champions. When I hit the winning homerun in the first of the two games I knew without a doubt that we were on our way to being the state's champions' man, gads, what a heady feeling that was let me tell you…

I can still hear the crack of the ball being slammed by my bat when the guy pitched it to me bud. When I saw that ball flying I didn't think twice. I simply dropped my bat and took off running the bases at what felt like it had to be at least ninety miles an hour… But somehow it also felt like I was running in slow motion. When I reached home-plate I was greeted by hard pats on the back, swats galore on my sexy tight ass and lots and lots of shoulder squeezes and pats on the head from my teammates. A few of the guys squatted down and grabbed my thighs and calves and hoisted me up to their shoulders. That was a truly heady feeling man; let me tell you, sitting up there on their shoulders. I felt like a king of sorts if you know what I mean. Gads, there's no better feeling for a baseball player than to be lifted by his buddies and carried off the field

on their shoulders. And all the while being up on my teammate's shoulders the sounds of the crowd cheering and calling
out my name, man that was immense! Looking back on it now
and seeing as you've made a souvenir of my dress socks Mr.
Kujman I recall a lot of the guys grabbing at my long socked
calves as I sat up there on my teammate's shoulders. I was
wearing navy blue thick baseball socks up to my calves, my
lucky socks actually. Every time I wore those stinkers we won a
game. And fuck, I never washed 'em either, I've heard where its
bad luck for a baseball player to wash his lucky socks until the
season is over. I don't recall where I heard that but I do know
that it's been mentioned in baseball type movies and I do have
somewhat of a superstitious nature I suppose it could be said
here. And some of my buddies knew that I considered those
long stinkers my lucky socks so I supposed that was why they
were grabbing at them. And it was also because of those danged lucky smelly socks of mine that I found myself in tickle torture trouble... Anyway, my teammates carried me clear across
the field and into the smelly and man-scented locker room...
While I was still up there on my buddies' shoulders I was
sprayed with torrents of cheap champagne, swatted real hard
on the butt and one of the fraternity actives actually had his
wooden paddle in his locker. That dude treated me to a few
good hard swats with that danged paddle man... At first I found
it to be humiliating and all, seeing as it wasn't hell week or anything like that yet, but in the nature of the game and seeing as
it was all in fun I decided to play along and let the fraternity
active named Bart swat my sexy ass a few times but then, woe
is me, he yelled out "Hey you guys, how about some real good
hard swats for our hero of the game here?" I shook my head
"no" from side to side grinning from ear to ear, tryin' to play
along with the fun. All my teammates clapped and hooted at
the prospect of spanking the hero of the game. I was doomed I
thought somewhat miserably. My ass cheeks had more than
gotten to know Bart's paddle since I had pledged the fraternity.
I think that that sadistic faggot actually reveled in paddlin' me

every chance he got. And now with my baseball uniform all soaked and sweaty and saturated with champagne he would have yet another chance at paddlin' his pledge. My buddies put me down and as they hooted and cheered and as Bart stood there with the paddle in hand, a mean looking glint in his eyes, I found myself doing a stupid sexy dance and then slowly rolling my uniform pants down in the back, exposing my creamy white butt cheeks. I figured at that point that it was best to go along with the fun and the locker room antics. I mean, how bad could a few swats to my sexy ass cheeks be bud? I bent over and Bart rubbed that dang paddle over my sexy whipped cream like butt cheeks, yelling out, "Who the fuck has dice? Give me a number for our hero here!" Fuck, there I was in the danged locker room with my pants pulled down with my damned sexy butt on display and this guy couldn't decide on how many fucking swats to give me. All I needed at that moment was for the coach to happen to walk into the locker room and find his star boy player with his pants pulled down in back, showing off what was left of the marks on my ass cheeks from the last time Bart had paddled me, which wasn't all that long ago either let me tell you. I heard one of my baseball buddies say that he had dice in his locker, seeing as he was a gamblin' man from time to time. I was reminded by Bart that if the dice landed on double digits that I would be treated to double the amount shown. (In other words if two fives were rolled I would get twenty swats rather than ten.)

"Fuck man, this is no way to be treating the hero of the game!" I hollered enthusiastically, knowing that this was all in fun so what the fuck.

"Fuck that buddy, this is the best way to be treating the hero of the game," Bart responded and gave me a good hard swat on the ass, just for my remark and I suppose to get things going. "And even though you're the hero of this game today I just want to make sure to keep you up to date on your status as a fraternity pledge and on whom your fraternity master is buddy boy..."

"OUUUCHHHHH!!!" I bellowed; my hands placed on my knees as I stood there stupidly bent over, mooning all my baseball buddies. "Yep Sir, that would be you Bart my man, my fraternity master!!"

The dice were rolled and the guys were all clapping and cheering, really whooping it up...

I gulped hard when I saw that the guy with the dice had rolled two sixes on the floor.

"Ah shit!!!" I ranted now, not having expected that awful turn of events.

"Holy crow Hotshot, check it the fuck out, double sixes for you," Bart hooted happily, rubbing that blasted paddle hard against my butt cheeks. "That means twenty-four swats. And to really liven things the fuck up here, not to mention that ass of yours I want you to choose five of your best buddies here to give you twenty-four swats each, including me... Heh!!"

"Wh-what???" I blurted, doing a quick calculation in my head. "But that would add up to one hundred and forty four swats Bart, I mean Sir!!"

"Very good Hotshot, at least we know you're going to pass math," the fraternity master chuckled and brought the paddle down hard on my butt cheeks.

"OUUCCHHH!!!" I screamed at the suddenness of it. "One Sir!!!"

Since I had pledged the fraternity I knew well enough to

count off each swat I received and to follow it with the word Sir. Bart brought the paddle down hard a second and third time…

"OWWWWWW!!! Two Sir, three Sir!!" I blurted.

Actually, this was the first time since I'd pledged the fraternity that Bart was paddling me in front of my baseball buddies. It was humiliating yet intoxicating somehow at the same danged time. All the guys in the locker room hooted and cheered me on as Bart delivered blow after stinging blow to my ass cheeks with his trusty paddle. Some of my good buddies were even yelling out things like "Paddle that sexy ass of his," and "Hey Merrick, you got a sexier butt than my girlfriend!" It was all in locker room fun and I did my best to deal with it all. By the time Bart reached the twenty-fourth swats my ass cheeks were pretty red, just as they were most of the time. It was never a big surprise for Bart and a couple of his fraternity underlings to show up at my dorm at the oddest times just to administer a good old fashioned paddling to my butt cheeks… Bart explained how he was teaching his underlings the art of disciplining and paddling a lowly pledge like me. He also went on to explain to me that he didn't have to explain a thing to me, that I had pledged the fraternity, that he was the pledge master and I was his to do with what he wanted, when he wanted. I sort of got the feeling that Bart had a thing for my sexy butt cheeks, and seeing as I had pledged the fraternity I knew that I had to deal with it, seeing as he always reminded me of how he was the fraternity master… I think Bart really had some kind of crush on me and paddling my ass was the only way that he could show how much I meant to him.

"Okay Hotshot, looks like those twenty four swats that I gave you got your ass cheeks all warmed up," Bart said, caressing my reddened cheeks with the paddle. "Now, have you chosen five buddies for the follow-ups?"

"S-sure thing Bart Sir," I replied, glancing up at my team-mates gathered around me.

I quickly sang out five of my best buddies' names and they all looked extremely elated to have been chosen... I sup-posed for them that swatting the hero of the game's ass cheeks was just another way of congratulating him. As they each took their turns to give me twenty four good swats each I stayed bent over in the assumed position bud. Bart quickly reminded me of the rules, how if I missed one number while counting off the swats I was receiving I would have to start back at the number one for the guy who was presently pad-dling me. The sounds of that paddle connecting stingingly and meanly with my ass cheeks started to get louder and louder and echoed through the locker room as my buddies really pum-meled the tar outa me...

The guys who I hadn't chosen to paddle me hooted, hollered, and clapped real loud amid the other sounds, the sounds of me saying "OUCH OUCH OUCH" over and the fuck over...

By the time the fourth guy got to his turn to paddle my ass cheeks they were redder than a fire engine let me tell you. The dude took up position behind me almost like a batter in a baseball game and began giving me the allotted swats... "OUCH!!! One!!!" I barked.

I didn't have to yell out "Sir" when my buddies paddled me that was reserved only for the fraternity master...

"WHOOOOO!!! Best way to celebrate after winning a game huh Merrick?" the dude paddling my red ass asked me. "OUCCHHH!!! Gads, if you say so," I stammered, starting to feel angry at this point, seeing as the guy was increasing the pressure with each blow when he spanked me.

By the time the spanking session was over my teeth were clenched good and tight and admittedly I was choking back tears, but I managed to smile through it all as my team-mates again congratulated me on a great game and Bart patted me on the back for being such a good sport about it all as I straightened up. As I stood there rubbing my red ass cheeks Bart also commented on how he just knew that I was going to do real well when "Hell Week" rolled around. From the sadistic look in his eyes I knew that Bart wasn't going to make "Hell Week" all that easy an experience for me. But before I could hike my uniform pants back up again in the back one of my stronger buddies, a guy named Jared sidled down between my legs and I suddenly found myself a few seconds later sitting up on his huge broad shoulders as I was again sprayed with torrents and torrents of champagne. A few of the guys even aimed for my mouth, making me guzzle some of the bubbly. It was warm and tasted like piss let me tell you. (And the only reason I can say that now is because of the fact that that wacky inventor had forced me to drink my own piss earlier. Gads, of all the fucked up things to happen to an attorney…) My strong buddy Jared carried me effortlessly around the locker room amid the clapping and cheers and hoots and hollers and all the ongoing locker room festivities… My cock was hard in my uniform pants at that point bud. (Fuck, every time Bart paddled my sexy ass cheeks I got all hard in the crotch…) If my buddy lugging me around the locker room felt my boner on the back of his head he made no mention of it bud… But it was when my so called buddy named Mike reached up and took one of my cleats off my smelly feet, poured some champagne in it and drank the danged champagne from it that all my tickle trouble started… At the words about my buddy Mike drinking champagne from my rancid smelling cleat Mr. Kujman's eyes seemed to really light up man…

"Ah, so now we get to the good stuff as they say eh Mr.

Merrick?" he asked me and stood up, stepping over to the lever that controlled the upper part of the device I was strapped into.

He pushed the lever and my upper body was laid back even more-so.

"Wh-what are you doing?" I asked my blasted client.

"Just making you a tad more comfortable Mr. Merrick," he replied as I was lowered and stretched out even more. "I want you to be very comfortable when you tell me this part of your tickle tale."

"Ahhhhhhhh gads," I grunted as my chest and pecs were pulled real taut.

Within a few seconds I found myself lying back so far that I was now looking up at the ceiling from a diagonal position, my big Adam's apple very pronounced and bobbing in my throat as I spoke...

"Okay then Mr. Merrick, you may continue now," the inventor said, sitting back down next to the device.

"Okay, where was I?" I said miserably. "Dang, oh yeah, my so-called buddy Mike drinking champagne from my cleat..."

"Why do you call him your so called buddy Mr. Merrick?" Mr. Kujman asked me, sounding overly curious.

"Well, mostly because of all the damned practical jokes he liked playing on me," I replied. "Not to mention that he stole my lucky socks that day in the locker room and if I wanted them back I had to submit to a long session of tickle torture..." At those words I gulped hard and again Mr. Kujman's eyes lit up...

Well, in the locker room as I sat atop my buddy Jared's shoulders there wasn't all that much I could do as Mike untied the laces on one of my rancid cleats and slid it off my smelly socked foot.

"Hey man, what are you doing down there?" I laughed, clapping my hands together.

My buddy who had me up on his shoulders laughed meanly. He grabbed my socked ankle real tight, leaned his head down and pressed the arch section of my foot against his nose. He inhaled deeply and grimaced miserably.

"WHEW, for a baseball hero this guy's feet really stink," Jared laughed and all the guys in the locker room hooted and howled as well.

"Fucked up way to talk about my danged feet and lucky socks!" I called out, laughing right along with all my baseball buddies.

As he held tight to my ankle Jared's hand moved down to the bottom of my foot and when he pressed his fingers against that section of my foot I nearly flew off his shoulders. "H-hey man, ha, ha, ha, ha, ha, ha, ha, ha, ha, ha, ha, be care-ful down there," I said laughingly. "My big ol' feet are mighty ticklish!"

"Ah, just the sort of thing I wanted to hear," my so called buddy named Mike said as he held up the cleat he had taken off my foot and in his other hand held up a bottle of the warm champagne that they had all been showering me with. "Gentlemen, there is an old legend in the annals of baseball history that if you drink from a hero player's stinky cleat you too will become a hero baseball player!"

"Ha, that ain't no danged legend!" I yelled down at my buddy as he poured the bubbly into my cleat. "Holy shit and fucking tarnation, he's really goin' to do it you guys! Shit, and let me tell you, my damned feet stink up my cleats like nobody's fucking business!"

"I'll say they do buddy," Jared laughed as he held me balanced on his shoulders and again leaned down and sniffed one of my socked feet. "Phew!!"

Fucking sleazy guy that he was Mike chugged down that champagne like it was the best tasting stuff on God's green Earth. As he drank we all clapped, cheered and hooted and Bart even gave my still exposed red ass a few extra swats with his trusty paddle while I sat perched up there on my buddies' shoulders. Mike refilled my cleat three more times and chugged down that awful champagne. And I have to tell you man, watching him do that made my boner even harder in my baseball uniform pants. But still my buddy Jared holding me up there on his shoulders didn't say anything at all...if he even noticed it that is...

"And gentlemen, there is one other legend that I wish to tell all of you about and then we can all get the fuck out of this stinking locker room," Mike went on, chucking my champagne scented cleat to the floor and started unlacing my other one.

"Hey, what now man?" I asked down at him from my perch up on Jared's shoulders. "You planning to drink out of that cleat next? Dang it man, you're goin' to be punch drunk by the time this is all over bud..."

From the look on Mike's face I got the distinct feeling that he hadn't truly enjoyed drinking from my danged cleat. I started figuring out too late that the guy had simply needed a reason to get my cleats off my feet.

"The other legend gentlemen is that if you are fortunate enough to somehow, and I mean somehow seeing as it's not that easy a task to pull off, but, if, if you are able to obtain a hero baseball player's socks then you too will become a great baseball player as well, Mike chuckled and in a fast move reached up, grabbed the tops of my socks, slipped his fingers into them and slid the long stinkers off me, baring my rancid feet.

"H-hey man, what do you think you're doin'?" I yelled down at my so called buddy and my buddy holding me on his shoulders purposely tickled the bottoms of my feet this time, holding me tight up there at the same time though. "Ha, ha, ha, ha, ha, ha, ha, ha, ha, ha, ha, ha, ha, ha, gads, t-told you I was ticklish man!! Ha, ha, ha, ha, ha, ha, ha, ha, ha, ha, ha, ha!!! Give me back my socks Mike! Those are my danged lucky socks you sleazy guy!!"

"All the more reason I want 'em buddy," Mike laughed and headed toward the back door of the locker room, holding up my socks in a dangling position. "If you want 'em back so badly buddy you know where my dorm room is..."

I watched as he bunched up my socks, stole a mean and hearty sniff from them and then he was gone, with my danged lucky socks of all things...

"Put me the fuck down!!" I ranted at my buddy Jared. All my teammates saw just how very, very pissed off I truly was at that moment Mr. Kujman, let me tell you...

"Ah, so that would explain your obvious anger at me having taken your socks as a souvenir of all this," the inventor said, waving his hand at me and the device that I was trapped in.

"I reckon," I said, sounding very Texan at that moment. "I mean, how can you blame me for being pissed off? I mean, how many guys out there have had their danged smelly socks stolen, and right off their feet no less, and twice in their life at that?"

"But please, continue," Mr. Kujman said.

"Okay, where was I now?" I asked no one in particular.

After Mike walked out of the locker room with my danged lucky socks my buddy Jared put me down from his shoulders. Judging from the look on my face none of my teammates, or even Bart my fraternity master approached me as I walked angrily toward my locker, my uniform pants still pulled down in back, and my reddened butt on total display...

"Fuck, fuck, of all the blasted things, goddamned guy steals my danged lucky socks!!" I ranted, giving my locker a hard punch. "How the fuck does he expect us to win the next games if I ain't wearin' my lucky socks???"

I didn't even shower, I was that pissed off. I just punched my locker again, got myself dressed and headed back to my dorm room all sweaty and stinky, the feeling of my sneakers on my feet with no socks very strange indeed...

That evening, around six AM, when all classes were done for the day I went to Mike's dorm room on a hunt of sorts for my lucky socks... I angrily knocked on his door...

"Come on in Merrick, I know that's you," Mike called from in his dorm room. "The door is unlocked buddy..."

With a look of out-right anger on my face I stepped into Mike's room. He was lying stretched out on his bed, clad in just a pair of white boxer shorts, the tip of his semi hardness peeking out of the fly opening. If he knew that he was on display in that fashion he made no mention of it whatsoever, and neither did I man, neither did I. A sports magazine was lying on the bed at his side. Obviously he had been reading and cast the magazine aside when I came knocking… But at the time I didn't make the connection between the sports magazine and the fact that my so called buddy was sporting a semi hard-on… "What can I do for you buddy?" he asked me snidely, turning on his side and looking at me almost hungrily.

"As if you didn't know, buddy," I replied in a seething tone. "Where are my danged lucky socks? We got another game tomorrow and I need those stinkers man! That was a shitty and fucked up thing to do man to steal my socks off me while Jared had me sitting up on his shoulders."

"Oh, they're around somewhere, tucked into a plastic zip lock bag and reeking bud, totally fucking reeking," Mike replied with a laugh-like sneer on his face. "Don't you ever wash those damned stinkers?"

"You know as well as I do that its bad luck for a baseball hero to wash his socks when he's on a winning streak," I replied angrily. "Now where are they Mike?"

Mike simply smiled meanly at me…

"Man, I'll tear this room apart to find them," I said angrily, taking a few steps toward him. "You've played some mean tricks on me in the past Mike, but this one has to be the meanest. You know I need those socks to help us win the next few games. Now where the fuck are they?"

"Well, as I said, they're around somewhere, but quite possibly not here in this room after all," Mike chuckled and got to his feet and faced me, his semi hardness now back in his danged boxer shorts.

The guy was awash with muscles, his whole body looked to be totally rock hard Mr. Kujman, a work of musculature art actually. I never knew the dude worked out so danged much...

"Not here in this room?" I asked him in disbelief. "What'd you do with 'em man?"

"Now take it easy buddy," Mike laughed. "Fuck it all buddy, never knew that a dude could get so worked up over a pair of his smelly and rancid socks. You'll get your socks, on one condition."

"And what the fuck might that be?" I asked him, taking another step toward him.

He simply smiled fiendishly, glanced down at my feet and then over at his bed...

"Oh no man," I whispered, quickly recalling the look on his face when he had discovered how ticklish my feet were back in the locker room.

"They're your socks man, how badly do you want them back?" Mike asked me teasingly and still looking over at his bed I saw the pile of rope on the floor. "It's no problem at all for me to keep them in that zip lock bag man, and that way they're no use to you whatsoever."

"Give me my lucky socks man," I said, practically pleading now.

"And just think buddy, someday if you're ever a famous baseball player I can auction those stinkers of yours off on E-bay," Mike laughed.

"Dang it all man, I don't need three guesses to know what the fuck you want," I grunted angrily.

"At least forty five minutes worth of tickle torture buddy," Mike said meanly. "Or a minimum of an hour, perhaps even ninety minutes at the most…"

I gulped hard, not wanting to submit to such a thing but already unbuttoning my white cotton button-down shirt…

"You sick bastard, you stole my socks just so you would be able to blackmail me into this shit?" I asked him in disbelief. "Fuck it all and tarnation man, I shouldn't have reacted so badly when I was up on Jared's shoulders and he accidentally tickled my danged foot."

"Like I said buddy, they're your socks," Mike said snidely and grinned at me as I took off my shirt, revealing my well toned muscular (at the time still pretty hairless) chest. "How badly do you really want them back?"

I shucked my sneakers off my feet, revealing the fact that I still hadn't put on new socks that day…

"I mean, you really don't believe that they're your lucky socks do you?" Mike asked me as I angrily unhitched my belt. "Do you really think that without wearing those socks we don't have a chance of winning the next few games buddy?"

The scent emanating from my danged feet was

immense in his small dorm room man, good laws it sure was... "Do you honestly believe that it's your smelly ol' socks that are helping us win the games buddy, and not just good baseball players working as a team?" Mike chided me.

"Just go ahead and do your worst man," I drawled angrily and let my khaki pants fall down around my ankles. "But after you're done I want my damned socks..."

I hadn't answered his questions where my beliefs about wearing my lucky socks helping us win games were concerned. I felt that was none of the joker's business. The fact remained pure and simple. He had stolen my damned socks and I wanted them back... Mike smiled from ear to ear as I stepped out of my khakis and shucked my under shorts off...

"Man oh fucking man, you really do believe that wearing those smelly ol' socks wins the games for us," Mike said, grabbing some rope and gesturing toward the bed as I stood there in all my muscular and naked glory, my danged Texas beef totally betraying me by plumping up hard as a rock. "You stripped down faster than a whore on a busy Saturday night." At that point in my tirade Mr. Kujman held up a hand to stop me momentarily...

"So let me understand this Mr. Merrick," the inventor said to me. "All in the interest of retrieving the socks your buddy had stolen from you did you submit to being tickle tortured by him?"

"You could say that I suppose," I replied, looking miserably at the inventor from my strapped down perspective. "And from what you're telling me you submitted totally willingly, there was no struggle between you and he," Mr. Kujman stated wonderingly, sounding like he was practically analyzing me. "Nope, none whatsoever," I said.

"And you really did believe that it was those socks that were aiding your team in winning the games?" the inventor asked me.

"It's just an old baseball superstition Mr. Kujman," I said helplessly. "But I didn't want to take any chances you know what I mean?"

"So you agreed to be tickle tortured," he said in total amazement now. "Knowing, knowing just how very ticklish you are…"

"I wanted my socks back," I said sheepishly, wondering as Mr. Kujman was if there were some other underlying reason of why I had agreed to Mike's terms, I mean, like most guys I had tons of socks after all.

Mr. Kujman nodded…

"Had I told you what my device was when you arrived here would you still have volunteered to be the participant in it, as you are now?" Mr. Kujman asked me.

I found that I hesitated an iota of a second before replying…

"Dang it all, no, no way man," I replied and turned my face away from him, looking up at the ceiling miserably as I lay there, totally helpless. "No way in hell Mr. Kujman!!"

"You may continue with your story Mr. Merrick," the inventor said, a knowing smirk on his face.

"Okay, now, let me just get my thoughts in order here," I began again.

Mike wasted no damned time in getting me lashed real fucking tight to his dorm room bed. As his good luck would have it and my bad luck would have it the guy had a double bed in his room, fucking queen sized at that... He instructed me to lye down on my back and to stretch myself out in a "X" spread-eagled type of position. He then lashed my wrists to the ends of the bed board, thus exposing my deep rank and some-what hairy armpits. He wasn't all that gentle about it either let me tell you, stretching my arms out good and fucking tight before lashing them to his bed board at the wrists. That done he stepped slowly over to my smelly and moist bare feet and got busy lashing them with mounds of rope at the ankles and tying them off to the legs of the bed. As he tied my first foot Mike leaned down and sniffed heartily at it, grazing his nose and lips over my danged rancid toes.

"Fucker, lookit you, just lookit you sniffin' and lickin' at my smelly ol' feet like the dog you are man," I grunted angrily. With a grin on his face as he tied up my other foot Mike gave the bottom of it a good hearty lick and slurp, sending ticklish thrills through me...

"H-hey, ha, ha, ha, ha, ha, ha, ha, ha, ha, ha!!" I laughed softly. "Gads, that tickles already, fuck, lick tickling me too???"

"Well, I'm sure you recall back in the locker room how I mentioned the legend of drinking out of a baseball player's smelly cleat and the legend of obtaining a baseball player's lucky socks?" Mike asked me snidely, looking me over from the foot of his bed as I now lay there totally helpless.
"Yeah, I remember," I replied. "What of it?"

"Well, a third legend and the most important one of all is that if one gets to lick a great baseball player's bare feet then he too will become a great baseball player," Mike said and stepped over to his dresser.

"Oh fuck all that legend shit Mike," I drawled miserably. "Those ain't no legends and you know it buddy. You just seem to be faggot for my danged feet..."

At my remark we both laughed, but then the laughter stopped when Mike opened his dresser drawer, reached in and when he turned around he was holding up two long peacock feathers...

"Oh fuck, oh no man," I gulped hard.

Smiling meanly Mike slowly approached the bed...

"Remember buddy, at least forty five minutes to an hour, at the most an hour and a half," Mike reminded me. "And then you'll get your lucky smelly socks back."

"Ha, okay man, like I said, do your worst!" I said, sounding snide now. "But I got one question for you buddy."

"What's that?" Mike asked in reply.

"Well, you got two big ol' feathers there," I said.

"Yeah, so?" Mike replied again in question.

"Well, the way you got me all tied and spread out like there ain't no way you'll be able to tickle both my feet at the same time man," I stupidly said. "There's no way that you can reach across that distance."

"I knew that he would wonder about that," Mike said, looking over at his clothes closet.

"Wh-wha..."I gasped when I saw the closet door open and my buddy Jared, the one who had carried me on his shoulders around the locker room step out.

Smiling fiendishly, he said hello to me, stepped over to Mike and took the other feather in hand. The look on my face at that moment was one of astonishment and shock.

"Me and my big mouth," I whispered miserably.

"Now you didn't think that I would miss this ho-down did you buddy?" Jared asked me, holding up the feather. "After finding out in the locker room that you were a ticklish dude and all? No way buddy..."

"Oh man Jared, and I thought we were good buddies," I snorted miserably.

"I can't believe that he let you get him all stripped and tied up like this," Jared said to Mike and my two so called buddies smiled fiendishly at each other. "I guess you were right when you said that he would do any fucking thing to get his stinky socks back."

"Well, I didn't strip him," Mike said. "As you heard from inside the closet he took care of that all by himself. He wants those lucky smelly socks of his so badly that he'll do any fucking thing to get 'em back..."

Lying there all tied up, totally naked and my Texas beef as hard as a rock in front of my two good buddies was more humiliating than I can attest to let me tell you.

"Just a few more moments and then we'll get started," Mike said, stepping over to his night table and opening the lower drawer.

I turned my head and watched as he took a plastic zip-lock bag out of the drawer and held it up. Gads, in that bag were my stinky lucky navy blue baseball socks.

"Now remember, these are the stinkers' up for grabs guys," Mike said, waving the bag around so that Jared and I could see. "One pair of lucky baseball socks, and may I say Byron that your feet really do fucking stink man!!"

He and Jared laughed meanly and I watched as Mike slit the top of the bag open and he and Jared each sniffed the contents heartily, grimacing and saying things like "Whew" as they sniffed my smelly baseball socks.

"Fuckers," I grunted angrily.

Then, Mike slid the zip-lock shut again and left the bag atop his night table, within my view.

"My danged socks," I said miserably, turning and looking up at my two buddies. "My fucking danged lucky socks..."

"Yeah, and I still can't believe just how fucking easy it was to get those smelly things off your feet buddy," Mike said laughingly.

"You bastards, you guys planned that didn't you?" I asked them, glancing back and forth at them and my socks in the zip-lock bag. "That's why you hoisted me up on your shoulders Jared, you muscled freak, so that Mike could get at my feet more easily..."

"Looks like he figured it out man," Jared said to Mike as I looked woefully at the zip-lock bag with my socks in it.

Fuck it all, my socks had been within my reach the whole time. All I'd had to do was push Mike aside and search the only place in the room where a pair of socks might be, in a sock drawer of all places...

"Now, you can get out of this any time you want Byron," Mike said, hunkering down at my left foot and taking a few hearty sniffs of it. "PHEW!!! Fucking stinky feet man! You just say the words "I've had enough" and we'll stop ticklin' you." "Yeah sure, and then I don't get my lucky socks back right?" I asked him angrily.

"Righty ho," Mike laughed as Jared hunkered down at my right foot.

"Shall we begin?" Mike asked Jared.

"I can't see any reason why not," Jared replied happily and then my two buddies began scrapin' the tips of those danged feathers against the bottoms of my very ticklish feet.

"Ohhhhhhhhhhhhhhhhrrrrrrrrr, no, no, ha, ha, ha, ha, ha, ha, ha, ha, ha, ha, ha, ha, ha, ha, ha, ha, ha, ha, ha, ha, ha, ha!!!!!!!" I roared in sudden and very loud laughter. "Ohhhhhhhhhhhhrrrrrr gads, of all the fucked up things!!! Ha, ha, ha, ha, ha, ha, ha, ha, ha, ha, ha, ha, ha, ha, ha!!!!!"

As I laughed and laughed like crazy they trailed the sides of the feathers between my toes a few times each, gads that was totally maddening. They held my feet immobilized by the upper sections of them and then tickled the beyond sensitive skin of my heels and then moving the feather tips slowly along my sexy arches.

"Ha, ha, ha, ha, ha, ha, ha, ha, ha, ha, ha, ha, ha, ha, ha!!!!" I laughed and laughed.

"So this is a baseball legend too Mike?" Jared asked his sadistic buddy. "Are there any old superstitions when it comes to tickling a baseball player's feet?"

"You mean like drinking from a baseball player's cleat or snagging his lucky socks?" Mike asked and tickled the bottom of my left foot more and more with the feather tip. "I don't think so; I think this is just more in fun when it comes to baseball players."

"Some fucked up fun this is, ha, ha, ha, ha, ha, ha, ha, ha, ha, ha, ha, ha, ha!!!" I chortled.

My two buddies laughed right along with me at Mike's snide remark...

"But man, lickin' a baseball player's feet, now that's the stuff that legends are made of buddy," Mike said to Jared and I could not believe what happened next Mr. Kujman.

The inventor looked at me intently as I went on and on with my story of my college days...

They stopped tickling my feet with the feathers (momentarily) and Jared watched as Mike stuck his tongue out and with the very tip of it began licking the bottom of my moist and smelly left foot.

"Ohhhhhhrrrrrrr!!!!! Ha, ha, ha, ha, ha, ha, ha, ha, ha, ha, ha, ha, ha!!!!" I chortled like crazy.

"Fuck man, you're lickin' his stinkin' foot," Jared said in awe as Mike grabbed my toes real tight, pressed his tongue harder against the bottom of my foot, slobbered like crazy all over it and tickled me by slurping up his saliva.

"Ha, ha, ha, ha, ha, ha, ha, ha, ha, ha, ha, ha, ha, ha, ha, ha, ha, ha!!!! Fuck lickin' my danged foot Jared, that bastard is lick ticklin' me!!" I guffawed crazily.

"Try it man, his feet stink, but at the same fucking time they somehow taste like magic," Mike said, glancing over at Jared. "Licking a great baseball player's feet is the stuff that true legends are made of man..."

Jared put his feather down on the floor beside Mike's, shrugged and with a nonchalant look on his face followed suit by doing with my right foot what Mike was doing with my left one, namely lick tickling it...

"Ha, ha, ha, ha, ha, ha, ha, ha, ha, ha, ha, ha, ha, ha, ha, ha, oooooooooooooooo!!!! Ha, ha, ha, ha, ha, ha, ha, ha, ha, ha, ha!!!!" I laughed crazily as my buddies licked the fuck out of the bottoms of my feet with the very tips of their mangy tongues.

They squeezed and teased my toes, sliding their fingers in between the crevices of them, driving me crazier than crazy, tickle torturing my cheesy toes.

"Har, har, har, har, har, har, har, har, har, har!!!!" I cawed crazily in Mike's dorm room.

"Mmmmm, can't believe I'm doing this," Jared stated, pressing his tongue harder still against the bottom of my foot and trailing it slowly upwards. "Like you said Mike, his feet stink like crazy but at the same time they taste like magic."

"Har, har, har, har, har, har, har, har, har!!!!" I laughed insanely as my two good buddies licked and lapped at my feet. "G-guys, people walkin' by out in the hall will hear me!!!"

I figured by stating that fact that they would think twice and stop tickling me. I mean, what if someone called the dean and we were found like that? Three guys in a dorm room, one of those three guys just happening to be the college's star baseball player all tied up to a bed and being tickle tortured by two of his best buddies?

"Wh-what if someone or more people hear me??? Har, har, har, har, har, har, har, har, ha, ha, ha, ha, ha, ha, ha, ha, ha, ha, ha, ha!!!" I screamed crazily. "They-they'll come a knockin' Mike and wonder what the fucks goin' on in here!!! Ha, ha, ha, ha, ha, ha, ha, ha, ha, ha, ha, ha, ha, ha!!!"
"Good deal," Mike laughed and sniffed the bottom of my saliva soaked foot. "The more the merrier I say."

"Yeah, we'll let them tickle you too if they want to," Jared laughed and he and Mike quickly resumed lick tickling the bottoms of my poor feet, getting louder and louder squeals of laughter out of me...

About ten minutes later they were again tickle torturin' my danged bare feet with the peacock feathers, moving and swirling them all over both my feet at the same time. The feathers as they splayed along my arches sent tingling and unnerving sensations through my entire being. My big Texas beef was more than plumped up and harder than hard man... Neither of my buddies made mention of it though... As I laughed and laughed and guffawed and cackled and cawed and screamed I kept glancing over at my smelly socks in the zip lock bag, the reason I was allowing all this to be done to me...

"ARRRRRRRRRHHHHH!!!!! Ha, ha, ha, ha, ha, ha, ha, ha, ha, ha, ha, ha, ha, ha!!!!" I ranted, fucking the air with my pre cum dripping cock as my body bucked wildly on the bed. I balled my hands into big fists and chortled like crazy, spewing saliva from my mouth at that point.

"PPPPPFFFFTTTTT!!!" was the sound that escaped me then.

After a good half hour or so of ticklin' the very bejesus out of my poor feet Mike and Jared stopped; I thought I was getting a break. Ha, actually those two foot and tickle faggots were gearing up for the next phase of tickling me. It would also be the reason Mike started calling my man nips my danged titty tits…

"Oh man, listening to him laugh and cackle like that is music to my ears man," Mike said to Jared as my two buddies got to their feet, still holding the peacock feathers in their hands.

"You aren't planning on telling anyone about any of this right Mike?" Jared asked. "I mean, this is all in fun, and fuck man, we licked his feet for crying out loud."

"Hee, hee, hee, hee, hee, hee, hee, hee," I snickered from the bed, even though my two buddies weren't tickling me at the moment.

But fuck, I could still feel the danged sensations…

"Nah, all of this is strictly between us here," Mike said, looking down at my chest, but more namely looking down at my jutted up and fleshy man nips. "Oh fuck man; I just got a new and great fucking idea."

"What do you mean?" Jared asked Mike as my so called buddy moved to the center of the bed at the side.

"Yeah, what do you mean?" I echoed Jared angrily, wondering what the fuck Mike had in mind for me now.

"Look at his meaty titty tits man, all erect and pronounced like," Mike said, reaching down and giving one of hard, hard nubs a squeeze and twist.

"M-my titty tits?" I growled. "What the fuck man, besides my feet now you're faggot for my damned man nips too?" "Fuck man, his big ol' titty tits are hard like I can't believe man," Mike said to Jared. "My girlfriend's titties don't get this hard." My two buddies laughed meanly, stepped to the sides of the bed and with the very tips of those danged peacock feathers they began tickle torturing the tips of my man nips.

"HA, HA, HA, HA, HA, HA, HA, HA, HA, HA, HA, HA, HA, Ha, ha, ha, ha, ha, ha, ha, ha, ha!!!!" I screamed laughingly at the top of my lungs then. "N-not my man nips you guys!! Fucker, titty tits my ass!!!"

With looks of sadistic pleasure etched on their faces my two so called buddies tickle tortured my poor man nips… They moved those danged feathers to my pulsing cock and stuck the tips of them into my wide sexy slit. Damn that tickled and was painful at the same fucking time let me tell you. It wasn't long before the tickling became so intense that I pissed all over my big chest and stomach areas… That was more than mortifying let me tell you Mr. Kujman… But I suppose the way they were ticklin' my piss slit it was inevitable…

I glanced over at Mr. Kujman as he mulled over what I had just related to him…

"Did you get your socks back in the end?" the inventor asked me and I saw that he had my long Gold Toe brand socks in his hand.

'Y-yeah, I did," I replied and watched as the sleazy inventor sniffed my dress socks, a look of sheer ecstasy on his face. "After Mike and Jared tickle tortured my feet, my Texas beef and my man nips for more than the allotted time I walked totally exhausted back to my dorm room, wearing my lucky socks on my feet... I was happier than a pig in shit to have my socks back that I had just had to wear 'em for the walk back to my dorm room...

When those two fuckers untied me from the bed I grabbed that damned zip lock bag, took my smelly socks out of it and rolled them onto my feet faster than anybody's business. And yeah man, they were more than smelly, they stunk like crazy, real baseball player sweat and raunch all over them. Mike looked woefully sad as I got those socks back onto my feet and then stood up. Jared and Mike had tickle tortured me for a total of nearly two hours before they let me out of that dorm room, me all smelly of sweat and piss, but with my lucky socks back... But I get the distinct feelin' here that you won't be giving me back those dress socks of mine Mr. Kujman...
"Did you try to give them a little payback after they untied you and you got dressed?" Mr. Kujman asked me, not replying to my question where my dress socks were concerned.

"Nah, I just wanted to get back to my dorm room, knowing that I had gotten what I had gone there for," I told the inventor.

Mr. Kujman simply stared at me blankly, a knowing sort of look in his eyes and my eyes betraying me at the same time...
"Did your team win the game the next day because you were wearing your lucky socks?" the inventor asked me, getting to his feet and sliding my socks back into his pants pocket. "Sadly, no we didn't," I replied woefully. "So much for legends huh?"

At that response Mr. Kujman himself erupted into peals of laughter, mockingly telling me how I had endured Mike's and Jared's tickle torture session all for nothing...

My short tale now ended Mr. Kujman pulled on the lever of the machine and my upper body was slowly raised back into a seated position...

"Wh-what now?" I asked him, trying to sound as nonchalant as possible. "Are we done here? Is the demonstration over?"

Mr. Kujman looked at me as if I had just asked the most ridiculous of questions and again got the feathers situated against the bottoms of my feet...

"Oh no, no," I whimpered miserably.

Grinning, the inventor pressed the button on the egg shaped device at my feet and the feathers started spinning again against the bottoms of my poor bare and trapped feet...

"Ohhhhhhhhhrrrrrrrrrr fuuuuuucccckkkkk, ha, ha, ha, ha, ha, ha, ha, ha, ha, ha, ha, ha, ha, ha!!!!!" I cackled anew, watching as the twisted and sadistic inventor proceeded to get the round manicure buffers situated against my man nips again.

"Time to tickle your titty tits again," Mr. Kujman said, sounding beyond sadistic at that point.

I pursed my lips together in anger, also trying to squelch the sounds of my insane laughter as the feathers did their dirty work. But then, the manicure buffers were again spinning and spinning and spinning against my man nips. I laughed loudly like a hyena, activating the sound sensors, causing the things to spin faster and faster, thus tickle torturing me all the more...

"P-please Mr. Kujman!!! Ha, ha, ha, ha, ha, ha, ha, ha, ha, ha, ha, ha, ha, ha, ha, ha, ha, ha!!!!" I somehow managed to cry out, after he got the buffers tickling my poor balls again.
My cock was piss hard all over again man...

Then, using my long white handkerchief Mr. Kujman again blindfolded me...

"We're coming to a most intense and extreme part of the "Laff-o-matic" demonstration Mr. Merrick," the inventor said to me, standing behind me and squeezing my shoulders. "I'll let you laugh a while more and relieve you again of the need to piss because I want you to totally concentrate on what's coming soon..."

As he spoke and massaged my shoulders I laughed and laughed like an out of control hyena on steroids. The inventor sounded totally maniacal...

"I-I'll do my best Mr. Kujman, ha, ha, ha, ha, ha, ha, ha, ha, ha, ha, ha, ha, ha, ha!!!!!" I hardy har harred. "After all, ha, ha, ha, ha, ha, ha, ha, ha, as, as your attorney it's my job after all... Ha, ha, ha, ha, ha, ha, ha, ha, ha, ha, ha, ha, ha, ha!!!!

With that I again heard the sound of the electric toothbrush with the high-speed spinning soft bristles as the inventor moved it slowly and menacingly toward my hardness...

"Ohhhhhrrrrrrrrrrr gads, ha, ha, ha, ha, ha, ha, ha, ha, ha, ha, ha, ha, ha!!!!!" I screamed crazily as he massaged my hard and veiny cock with the whirling bristles and once again I was forced to shoot my load all over myself, all while laughing uncontrollably and to my death I thought miserably…

"HA, HA, HA, HA, HA, HA, HA, HA, HA, OOOOOOOOOOOO FUCK, makin' me cum this time before makin' me piss huh Mr. Kujman???" I blurted stupidly and the only other thing I could think of at that moment was if my wife could see her poor husband now… "Ha, ha, ha, ha, ha, ha, ha, ha, ha, ha, ha, ha, ha, ha, ohhhhhrrrrrrrr fuccckkk!!!" I grunted and laughed as I shot my load, feeling my warm juices splattering all over my upper body…

When I was done shooting my load Mr. Kujman turned off the electric toothbrush and even blindfolded I could feel his eyes riveted on me and watching as I laughed and bucked in his creation, his evil and fucked up creation bud…

"Hmmm, looks like I'll have to turn off the tickle devices so that you can relieve yourself again Mr. Merrick," the inventor said more to himself than to me it seemed.

When the tickle devices attached to the egg-shaped machines were turned off my squeals of laughter again died down, but slowly, so slowly bud, seeing as the sensations of being tickled were still coursing through me… But then, again, the awful ball shaped gag with the breathing hole in it was strapped around my neck and into my mouth. I gurgled miserably, knowing that the sadistic and prank playing inventor was about to make me drink my own piss…again… I squirmed miserably under the tight and binding straps as I felt the device called the "Ferguson Catheter" being fitted snugly over my bloated and sensitive feeling cock head.

"RRRRRRRR!!!!!" I gurgled against the ball gag in my mouth as I felt the thin rubber tube being inserted into the breathing hole.

"Alright then Mr. Merrick, please relieve yourself, and I will assure you that this will be the last time that I make you consume your urine," Mr. Kujman said to me, stroking my sheathed cock a few times to get my stream going.

"PFFFTTTTTT!!!" I sputtered miserably into my ball gag as the first droplets of my piss filled my mouth.

As I sat there in blindfolded darkness making glubbing sounds I scoffed down my rancid piss a second time and heard the unmistakable sound of my camera clicking away. Good gads and good laws man, that inventor was snapping pictures of me as I drank my danged rancid piss...

GLUB GLUB GLUB was the infernal sounds that I made as my cock seemed to bloat and deflate as it spewed forth my smelly stream... With that ball gag in my mouth I had choice but to keep my gullet wide open and swallow quickly as I was fed my piss... Fucked up and sick thing to do to an attorney wouldn't you say?

When I was done relieving myself the inventor quickly took the "Ferguson Catheter" off my poor swollen cock head and took the ball gag out of my mouth.

"Damn, damn, dang it all," I swore softly. "Made me drink my piss again!!"

"Yes, and now that you've relieved yourself Mr. Merrick it's time for another demonstation where my "Laff-o-matic" is concerned."

I had had more than my fill of demonstrations where the mad inventor's machine was concerned, but seeing as he had-n't yet un-strapped me from it I saw no way of getting out of what was coming next. I heard him place the "Ferguson

Catheter" and the ball gag back on the table and then Mr. Kujman went about the work of preparing me for the next round of tickle torture…

As I sat there helplessly strapped to the device and blindfolded I suddenly felt the sensation of a brush being slid up and down and all over my feet. I also felt that my feet were being slopped with some sticky liquidy-like stuff.

"Uh, M-Mr. Kujman, Sir, what are you doing now?" I asked the inventor. "Could you take this blindfold off me please? I, uh, really don't like not being able to see…"

"It's all part of the demonstration Mr. Merrick," the inventor stated sternly and I felt the brush with the sticky substance on it being moved between my toes, on my arches and all over the bottoms and tops of my bare feet.

It tickled as Mr. Kujman slopped whatever it was all over my feet with the brush but not as intensely as it had tickled when he was using his "Laff-o-matic" device on me. After he'd painted my feet with whatever it was more than liberally, more than five or six times I began smelling a very sweet scent in the air.

"Wh-what is that stuff you're coatin' my danged feet with?" I drawled, feeling anger more than anything at this point. "Hee, hee, hee, hee, hee, hee, hee, th-that brush you're usin' on me sure does tickle Mr. Kujman…"

"That's what this is all about after all my dear attorney, the art and the beauty of tickling a handsome young robust man…" the inventor said sadistically.

When he was done painting my feet with whatever the sweet scented sticky stuff was I heard the sound of a jar being put down on a table... Whatever the stuff all over my feet was it was dripping off me and landing on the floor. I heard the slight plopping sounds...

I then heard the sound of something being moved around the room and then I felt a warmth settle over my bare and sticky feet, as if they had been encased in something or other...

"Mr. Kujman, what's the point of all this?" I asked through clenched teeth, my blindfold sliding down toward my nose, blocking my sight even more, totally frustrating. "You've done your demonstration, and not to mention that you've done it to me. I would like to be let out of here at this point...please Sir..."

With that he whipped the blindfold off me and I took in the awful sight of what he had done and prepared my poor feet for... I saw that the warmth that I had felt engulf my feet was actually a heavy-duty plastic box mounted on a rollaway contraption of sorts. At one of the wheels on the bottom of it I saw a lock that held it in place for the way the inventor wanted it at the moment. The plastic box, like the square piece of wood that my feet were locked in had a big hole in it where my feet were encased, totally surrounding the piece of wood with my feet in it. On top of the plastic box was another hole with a cork-like stopper in it, this hole much smaller than the one accommodating my danged smelly feet. After all the sweating my big 'ol feet had done from being so relentlessly tickled I could only imagine how badly they were smelling up the inside of that blasted box that the inventor had encased 'em in. On a table I saw what Mr. Kujman had slopped and painted all over my feet. It was a jar of sweet honey with a basting brush next to it.

"Wh-what is this?" I asked the inventor as he stepped over to a cabinet mounted on a wall. "What are plannin' on doin' to me next here?"

I watched as he opened the cabinet and took out a long clear tube. As he stepped back over to me, holding up the tube I saw to my utter horror that crawling around in the tube were ants, thousands and thousands of ants...

I gulped hard and screamed like a woman...

The inventor chuckled meanly as he watched me struggling like a madman now to free myself from his infernal device of torture...

"This has gone far enough man!!" I roared mightily. "GADS, ohhhhhhhhhhh fuck, fuck, you slopped up my feet with honey you mad scientist inventor!!!"

Looking at my feet trapped in that see-thru box I saw just how very liberally and heavily the inventor had coated my danged tootsies. As I wiggled my toes honey slopped off them and dripped to the bottom of the box...

"Tell me Mr. Merrick, did you know that ants love honey?" the inventor asked me as he stepped over to the heavy-duty plastic box that my poor feet were encased in.

"N-no, I didn't know that man, nor do I give a flying fuck!!" I ranted. "Oh good God man, don't do what I think you're goin' to do, please man!!!"

"I must say, you chose the right profession as a lawyer Mr. Merrick," Mr. Kujman said, still chuckling as he pulled the stopper out of the top of the plastic box, baring the hole. You sure do figure things out rather quickly I would say."

As he spoke he mockingly imitated my Texas accent. I

then watched with my eyes open wide in terror as he took the small stopper out of the tube that the ants were in. I saw that the stopper had tiny air-holes in it.

"Mr. Kujman, no, no, this is unthinkable now," I blurted miserably as he held the open end of the tube over the hole in the plastic box. "Ohhhhhhhhhh g-gads, no, no!!!!"

I choked on my tears, watching as he shook the tube and the ants were forced out and into the box, some of them already landing on my honey slopped feet.

"They love the taste of honey and when they crawl through it a few hundred at a time the sensations can be ticklish and maddening at the same time," the inventor said, shaking the tube some more and causing the crawly critter insects to fall into the box.

With my lips pursed in agony I watched as the ants that fell to the bottom and the sides of the box quickly made their way over and onto my honeyed feet, joining the ants that had been lucky enough to land right on them.

"Ohhhhhhhhhh fuuuuuccccckkkk," I whimpered; the sensations as they crawled on my honeyed feet beyond maddening, beyond what the inventor had described.

I attributed the fact that my feet had been so thoroughly tickled that that was why they were so overly sensitized, not to mention the fact that the wacky inventor had forced me to shoot my load two danged times. Shooting my load always makes every damned part of me more than sensitive to the touch bud... As the ants crawled over and over my feet, along my arches, between my toes, up on my heels and the lucky ones on the beefy bottoms and tops of them I felt the tickling sensations beginning anew...

"Ha, ha, ha, ha, ha, ha, ha, ha, ha, ha, ha, ha, ha, ha, ha, ha, ha!!!!" I started laughing all over again, softly at first. "Ah good, we're back in business as they say Mr. Merrick," Mr. Kujman said happily, finished now with pouring the ants from the tube and into the box.

He stuck the stopper into the hole at the top of the box and stepped next to me as I chuckled softly, my laughing though getting louder with each passing second as the ants crawled all over my feet. What a sight that was let me tell you man, watching as my poor feet were slowly being covered with thousands of crawly ants…

"Ha, ha, ha, ha, ha, ha, ha, ha, ha, ha, ha, ha, ha, ha, ha, ha, ha, ha, ohhhhhrrrrrrr g-gads, that, that feels awful Mr. Kujman!!!" I screamed, and saw that once again the inventor had my camera out of my attaché case.

As the ants ate the honey off my danged feet and as I sweated and laughed my head off the inventor snapped more than a few pictures of me.

"Th-this is blackmail, and its torture," I blurted miserably as this time he did not return my camera to my attaché case. This time he stashed it in a wall safe. I laughed and laughed, swinging my feet around in the box as much as possible, trying to shake the ants off them as the inventor spun the combination and locked the wall safe… I would never get my camera back now I thought more than miserably…

"As I said those pictures will insure your silence about our little adventure here today Mr. Merrick," the inventor said, watching as the ants crawled over and over my poor feet. "And those pictures will also insure that you are now my demonstration associate whenever I want to show off my device to prospective customers..."

"Y-you've got to be joking you lunatic!!" I sputtered, spittle flying out of the sides of my mouth. "I'm a lawyer, not a damned guinea pig for your twisted invention!"

Without a word he simply glanced over at his wall safe and then looked at me.

"Ah shit," I grumbled and together we watched as the ants crawled over and over my feet.

As I twitched my toes I felt teeny tiny stings happening on the tender flesh between them...

"Har, har, har, har, har, har, har, har, har, har, ha, ha, ha, ha, ha, ha, ha, ha, ha, ha, ha, ha, ha, ha!!!!! OUCH!!!! OUCH!!!!" I laughed and ranted and laughed and ranted and laughed and ranted. "OUUUCCCCHHHHHH!!!! F-fucking ants are stingin' me man..."

"Not to worry Mr. Merrick, they're far from poisonous," the inventor chuckled meanly.

I looked at my captor with total dismay in my eyes as my feet itched and were tickled simultaneously. Then, with even more dismay showing in my eyes I watched as Mr. Kujman pressed the manicure buffers again against my man nips and my sweaty and stinky balls.

"Oh no, no, not this too," I gasped. "Ha, ha, ha, ha, ha, ha, ha, ha, ha, ha, ha, ha, ha, ha!!!!!"

With a sly look in his devilish eyes Mr. Kujman pressed the button on the egg shaped device and the buffers pressed against my sore nipples and aching balls came to spinning life.

"OHHHHHHHHRRRRRRR!!!!!" I roared. "HA, HA,HA, HA, HA, HA, HA, HA, HA!!!!!" was all I could say now as the buffers tickled me and the ants ate and stung at my honeyed feet.

My vision blurred at that point as I writhed and screamed in the throes of forced ecstasy…

Then, to really send me into orbit I could have sworn that I saw Mr. Kujman sticking a thin and pointy backscratcher through the hole in the top of the plastic box that my bare feet were encased in… And he started scratching the bottoms of my feet with it, shooing the ants off me a little at a time… I leaned my head back, swooned, laughed and laughed and laughed and laughed and eventually passed out… I think… When I opened my eyes the first thing I (happily) realized was that I was no longer strapped up to the infernal "Laff-o-matic" device. The plastic box was gone and so were the ants. Mr. Kujman was standing at the end of the machine wiping the honey off my feet with a damp cloth; I think that was actually what woke me bud.

"Feeling okay?" the inventor asked me.

"Y-yeah, I suppose so," I drawled in my Texas accent, running my hands over my sweat sopped face, glad to have the use of my hands again.

"So, are you ready to begin the paperwork or would you like another demonstration of my device, just to be sure you know exactly how it works?" Mr. Kujman asked me, squeezing one of my feet while he wiped it with the damp cloth.
I gulped hard as the inventor chuckled…

After getting all the paperwork done and the patent license finalized I allowed the inventor to drive me back to my office in his cheesy and hot car, but we made a stop at a men's clothing store where I purchased new socks and undershirts... Gads, wearing a pair of dress shoes with no socks sure does feel strange bud...

A Week Later

I had been made partner. The firm was now called "Richards, Gage, Sommers and Merrick. Because I had done so well on the deal with Mr. Lewis Kujman that was my reward, that and a huge commission check for my hard work. God, if only the top partners in the firm knew just what I had gone through to secure that deal and the huge fee for the firm. It seemed that the inventor knew about it after having spoken with Mr. Richards but as requested by the top partner in my firm he had kept the secret to himself. I was the happiest so and so on the planet buddy... Well, almost the happiest so and so. Leaning back in my chair behind my desk in my office, my wingtip shoed feet propped up atop my desk I was on the phone with my newest client, a client who had heard of my services through my last client...

"Uh yes Mr. Etuk, you say you've invented some kind of new device that performs erotic suctions and massages while tickling the recipient," I gulped as I spoke, trying to sound ecstatic at the same time. "And you want me there all day tomorrow to test it out for you eh Sir?"

My toes twitched in my shoes and when I hung up the phone I sat behind my desk looking at the pictures of myself in Mr. Kujman's "Laff-o-matic" device... There are a few pictures of me laughing my head off as the feathers are spinning against the bottoms of my bare feet, there are a few pictures of me having my man nips tickle tortured as well, laughing my head off in those too, but the ones where my big Texas pride and joy, my big beef is on display are truly the pictures that Mr. Kujman has me by the balls with so to speak. My cock is harder than hard in those pictures and from the way I'm laughing it sure does look like I'm rather enjoying myself while being tickled… Seeing pictures of myself all strapped up and sweating and laughing always causes my cock to rise for whatever the fuck the reason bud. I keep the pictures safely tucked away in my office safe, just as Mr. Kujman keeps the originals tucked away in his safe in his workshop where the device is, the device that he tricked me into and tortured me with, the device that I issued him a patent for. I stood up and walked slowly toward Mr. Richards' office to tell him that I would be meeting with a new client the next day, for the better part of the whole day actually…

I had no doubt that the top partner in my firm would be ecstatic to hear of the new business that I was bringing in, via our new client, Mr. Etuk…

ABOUT THE AUTHOR

Christopher Trevor was born in July 1963 and grew up in New York City. As soon as he was old enough to know how he began writing fiction and has been writing gay erotic/fetish stories for the past ten to twelve years at this point. He became an avid reader as well from the time he knew how and reads everything from fiction, to non-fiction to biographies of interesting and unusual people, people who have made a difference or who have paved the way for others. Christopher attributes his writing artistic inspiration to artists such as Etienne, Tom of Finland, Tagame, The Hun, and most notably Joe T, who Christopher has had the pleasure of  speaking with and even meeting over the last few years. Christopher states, "Joe T encouraged me to write about my fetish because I was embarrassed about it at the time. Joe T said that when we are embarrassed about something that makes it even more enticing somehow." Christopher totally agreed and never stopped writing in this genre. Erotic writers who inspired Christopher Trevor were: Tom Shaw (author of "That Day at the Quarry), C.S. White (author of Big Sur), Larry Townsend (author of countless erotic novels), and Mason Powell (author of the classic story "The Brig.")

Christopher discovered that not only did he enjoy writing erotic tales but that after his first bondage experience he had a genuine flair for it. Writing to erotic oriented magazines about his first bondage experience truly opened the floodgates for Christopher where this style of writing is concerned. Christopher thanks the handsome and muscular "Greg" for that experience way back in time. Christopher took "Creative Writing" courses every semester during his high school years and while other friends of his stopped writing what they loved to write about as time went on Christopher never let a day go by when he didn't write something... "I feel that if I don't write every day I will die," Christopher has said many times over.

Foot fetish stories and all things related; spanking fetish, erotic shaving, muscle bondage, tickle torture, and hardcore stories are just a few of the areas of gay eroticism that Christopher enjoys writing about and inspiring in others as well. As one internet buddy said to Christopher where the black socks fetish is concerned, "Until I started talking with you I never gave a thought to my socks when I got dressed for work in the morning. Now when I pull my dress socks on every morning I get a chill up my spine."

Christopher is proud of the erotic effect he has on people...

Christopher Trevor is also the author of:

> The Executive Guide to Foot Fetishism and Office Discipline
> 1-887895-36-1

> Executive Ties That Bind
> 1-887895-37-X

> Timmy And The Hong Kong Tailor
> 1-887895-30-2

Look for them where you found this book or Amazon.com

www.ingramcontent.com/pod-product-compliance
Lightning Source LLC
Chambersburg PA
CBHW071222260626
47162CB00004B/1393